"What can I do for you, Mr....?"

The question of his name hung in the warm air around them, testing and challenging him. Charlotte stood tall as his astonished gaze traveled down her body, taking in her disheveled appearance. Her skin tingled as those eyes all but caressed every part of her, making her breath catch as if he'd actually touched her.

"You are Sebastian's sister?" Accusation and disbelief laced every word, but it was lost on her, as the grief she'd thought she'd finally begun to get over hit her once more when he said her brother's name.

The urge to defend herself rose up, but she had no idea what from. "Yes," she said curtly, hearing the irritation in her own voice. "And you are?"

She asked the question, although she knew the answer, and it was not one she wanted to hear. She curled her fingers into her palms, knowing that the one man she'd never wanted to meet, the man she held responsible, first for taking Seb away from her, then for his death, was standing impudently in her garden. Looking for her.

Rachael Thomas has always loved reading romance and is thrilled to now be a Harlequin Presents® author. She lives and works on a farm in Wales, a far cry from the glamour of a Harlequin Presents® story, but that makes slipping into her characters' world all the more appealing. When she's not writing or working on the farm, she enjoys photography and visiting historic castles and grand houses. Visit her at rachaelthomas.co.uk.

Books by Rachael Thomas

Harlequin Presents

Claimed by the Sheikh
A Deal Before the Altar

Visit the Author Profile page
at Harlequin.com for more titles.

Rachael Thomas

———

Craving Her Enemy's Touch

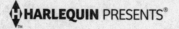
HARLEQUIN PRESENTS®

Recycling programs
for this product may
not exist in your area.

ISBN-13: 978-0-373-13819-7

Craving Her Enemy's Touch

First North American Publication 2015

Copyright © 2015 by Rachael Thomas

Printed in U.S.A.

Craving Her Enemy's Touch

For Ruth and Sarah Jane
and our enjoyable writing retreat weekends
in our little Welsh cottage.

CHAPTER ONE

THE PURR OF a sports car broke the quietness of the afternoon, taking Charlie's mind hurtling back to the past. To events she'd been hiding from for the last year.

She had grown up in the glamour of the racing world, but her brother's death had sent her retreating to the country and the sanctuary of her cottage garden. It was a place that was safe, but instinct warned her that this safety was now under threat.

Unable to help herself, she listened to the unmistakable sound of the V8 engine as it slowed in the lane beyond her garden, appreciative of its throaty restraint. All thoughts of planting bulbs for next spring disappeared as memories were unleashed. Images of happier times filled her mind, colliding with those of the moment her world had fallen apart.

Kneeling on the grass in the corner of her garden, she couldn't see the car on the other side of the hedge, but she knew it was powerful and expensive—and that it had stopped in the lane outside her cottage.

The engine fell silent and only birdsong disturbed the peace of the English countryside. She closed her eyes against the dread which rushed over her. She didn't need visits from the past, however well meaning. This unexpected visitor had to be her father's doing; he'd been pushing her to move on for weeks now.

The heavy clunk of the car door shutting was followed by purposeful footsteps on the road. A few seconds later they crunched on the gravel of her pathway and she knew that whoever it was would see her at any second.

'Scusi.' The deep male voice startled her more than the Italian he spoke and she jumped up as though she were a child with her hand caught in the sweet jar.

The six foot plus of dark Italian male which stood in her garden robbed her of the ability to think, let alone speak, and all she could do was look at him. Dressed in casual but very much designer jeans which hugged his thighs to perfection, he appeared totally out of place and yet vaguely familiar. Over a dark shirt he wore a leather jacket and was everything she'd expect an Italian man to be. Self-assured and confident, oozing undeniable sex appeal.

His dark collar-length hair was thick and gleamed in the sunshine, his tanned face showed a light growth of stubble, which only enhanced his handsome features. But it was the intense blackness of his eyes as they pierced into her which made breathing almost impossible.

'I am looking for Charlotte Warrington.' His accent was heavy and incredibly sexy, as was the way he said her name, caressing it until it sounded like a melody. She fought hard against the urge to allow it to wrap itself around her. She had to. She was out of practice in dealing with such men.

Slowly pulling off her gardening gloves, she became acutely aware she was wearing her oldest jeans and T-shirt and that her hair was scraped back in something which almost resembled a ponytail. Could she get away with not admitting who she was? But the arrogance in those dark eyes as they watched her made her want to shock him.

He was undoubtedly her brother's business partner, the man who had whisked him deeper into the world of performance cars, so far that he'd almost forgotten his family's existence. Indignation surfaced rapidly.

'What can I do for you, Mr...?' The question of his name hung in the warm air around them, testing and challenging him. She stood tall as his astonished gaze travelled down her body, taking in her dishevelled appearance. Her skin tingled as those eyes all but caressed every part of her, making her breath catch as if he'd actually touched her.

'You are Sebastian's sister?' Accusation and disbelief laced through every word, but it was lost on her as the grief she'd thought she'd finally begun to get over hit her once more as he said her brother's name.

The urge to defend herself rose up, but she had no idea where it came from. 'Yes,' she said curtly, hearing the irritation in her own voice. 'And you are?'

She asked the question although she knew the answer and it was not one she wanted to hear. She curled her fingers into her palms, knowing that the one man she'd never wanted to meet, the man she held responsible, first for taking Seb away from her, then for his death, stood impudently in her garden. Looking for her.

If that wasn't bad enough, there had been a spark of attraction in that first second she'd seen him. Already she hated herself for it. How could she feel anything other than contempt for the man who'd deprived her of her brother?

'Roselli,' he said and stepped off the path and onto her newly cut lawn, confirming her worst suspicions. He smiled at her as he walked closer, but it didn't reach his eyes. 'Alessandro Roselli.'

She glared at him and he stopped a few paces away from her. Had he felt the heat of her anger? She certainly hoped so. He deserved every bit of it and so much more.

'I have nothing to say to you, Mr Roselli.' She stood firm, looked him in the eye and tried not to be affected by the way his met and held hers, shamelessly, without any trace of guilt. 'Now, please leave.'

She walked across the lawn, past him and towards her cottage, sure that he would go, that her cold dismissal would be enough. As she neared him the breeze carried his scent. Pure, unadulterated male. Her head became light, her breath hard to catch. In disgust at the way he distracted her thoughts, she marched off.

'No.' That one word, deep and accented, froze her to the spot as if a winter frost had descended, coating everything in white crystals.

A tremor of fear slipped down her spine.

Not just fear of the man standing so close to her, but fear of all he represented. Slowly she turned her face to look directly at him. 'We have nothing to say. I made that clear in my response to your letter after Sebastian's death.'

Sebastian's death.

It was hard to say those words aloud. Hard to admit her brother was gone, that she'd never see him again. But, worse, the man responsible had the nerve to ignore her early grief-laden requests and then invade the cottage, her one place of sanctuary.

'You may not, but I do.' He stepped closer to her, too close. She held his gaze, noticing the bronze sparks in his eyes and the firm set of his mouth. This was a man who did exactly what he wanted, without regard for anyone else. Even without knowing his reputation she'd be left in no doubt of that as he all but towered over her.

'I don't want to hear what you've got to say.' She didn't even want to talk to him. He had as good as killed her brother. She didn't want to look at him, to acknowledge him, but something, some undeniable primal instinct, made her and she fought hard to keep the heady mix of anger and grief under control. An emotional meltdown was not something she wanted to display, especially in front of the man she'd steadfastly refused to meet.

'I'm going to say it anyway.' His voice lowered, resembling a growl, and she wondered which of them was fighting the hardest to hold onto their composure.

She lifted a brow in haughty question at him and watched his lips press firmly together as he clenched his jaw. Good, she was getting to him. With that satisfaction racing through her, she walked away, desperate for the safety of her cottage. She didn't want to hear anything he had to say.

'I am here because Sebastian asked me to come.' His words, staccato and deeply accented, made another step impossible.

'How dare you?' She whirled round to face him, all thought of restraint abandoned. 'You are here because of your guilt.'

'My guilt?' He stepped towards her, quickly closing that final bit of space between them, his eyes glittering and hard.

Her heart thumped frantically in her chest and her knees weakened, but she couldn't let him know that. 'It's your fault. You are the one responsible for Sebastian's death.'

Her words hung accusingly between them, and the sun slipped behind a cloud as if sensing trouble. She watched his handsome face turn to stone and even thought she saw the veil of guilt shadow it, but it was brief, swiftly followed by cold anger, making his eyes sharper than flint.

He was so close, so tall, and she wished she was wearing the heels she used to favour before her life had been shaken up into total turmoil. She kept her gaze focused on him, determined to match his aggressive stance.

'If, as you say, it was my fault I would not have waited a year to come here.' His voice was cool and level, his eyes, changing to gleaming bronze, fixed her accusingly to the spot.

He took one final step towards her, so close now he could have kissed her. That thought shocked her and she resisted the need to step back away from him, as far as she could. She hadn't done anything wrong. He was the guilty one. He was the one who'd intruded on her life.

'It was your car that crashed, Mr Roselli.' She forced each word out, his proximity making it almost impossible.

'Your brother *and* I designed that car. We built it together.' His voice, deep and accented, hinted at pain. Or was she just imagining it, reflecting her grief onto him?

'But it was Sebastian who test drove it.'

She fought the memories he was dragging up. Demons she'd thought she'd finally shut the door on.

He didn't say anything and she held her ground, looking up into his eyes as they searched her face. Her heart pounded wildly and deep down she knew it wasn't just the memories of Sebastian. It was as much to do with this man. Instinctively she knew his potent maleness had disturbed the slumbering woman hidden within her—and she hated him for that.

'It couldn't have done your company's reputation any good when an up-and-coming racing driver was killed at the wheel of your prototype.' She injected a jaunty edge to her words, issuing a challenge. At the same time she wished she could run and hide—from the memories he stirred as much as from the way her body reacted to each glance from his devilishly dark eyes.

He didn't move. He didn't flinch at all. He was in complete control as his eyes glittered, sharp sparks like diamonds spiking her soul.

'It wasn't good for anyone.' His voice was icy cold and, despite the warmth of the September sun, she shivered, but still he remained, watching as if he could read every thought that raced through her mind.

She drew in a ragged tear-laden breath and swallowed hard. She couldn't cry, not now. Not again. She was done with crying. It was time to move on, time to forge a new path through life. She couldn't go back to what she'd been doing before. Her time in front of the cameras, representing Seb's team, was over. The memories would be too much, yet this man seemed hell-bent on bringing the past into the present.

'I think you should leave, Mr Roselli.' She stepped away from him, out of his shadow and into the sun as it crept out from behind the clouds. 'Neither is it doing me any good.'

With eyes narrowed by suspicion, he watched her as she took another step back and away from him. 'I am here because Sebastian asked me to come.'

She shook her head, the emotional meltdown she'd wanted to keep at bay threatening to erupt. 'I still want you to leave.'

She didn't care if he remained standing in her precious garden; she just wanted to escape him, escape the aura of a man obviously used to getting all he wanted, no matter what the cost to anyone else.

Alessandro closed his eyes and sighed as Charlie fled across the garden, heading for the open door of the cottage. Hysteria had not been on his agenda. He didn't need this now. For a moment he thought about turning and walking away, getting in his car and driving as fast and as far away as he could. He'd kept part of his promise to Sebastian, after all. But had he even achieved that?

'Maledizione!' he cursed aloud and strode after her, his legs brushing against the lavender which tumbled from the borders, raising the scent. Just being in the garden, with its proud display of flowers, made him remember the time he'd looked after his sister while she'd recovered from a car accident. It was a memory that wouldn't help at all right now.

As he neared the open back door he heard Charlie's frustrated growl. He didn't knock, didn't pause. He just walked straight in. He wasn't going to be dismissed so easily.

This woman had stubbornly refused her brother's requests to go to Italy and see the car they'd been working on and it had angered him. Then, after the accident, he'd offered his support, but he'd never expected her rejection or her cold and furious denial of his existence.

With her arms locked rigidly tight, she leant on the kitchen table, her head lowered in despair. She spun round to face him. 'How dare you?' Hot angry words hurtled across the small space to him, but he stood tall, despite the low beams of the old cottage, and took her anger.

'I dare because I promised Sebastian that I would.' He moved nearer to the small table, nearer to her, until only a pulled-out chair, left as if recently vacated, separated them.

'I'm sure Seb would not have made anyone promise to come and hassle me like this.' He watched as her full lips clamped shut on further words and he felt the strangest desire to kiss those lips, to taste her rage and frustration, to draw it from her and replace it with hot desire.

'Hassle?' He frowned at her and saw her green eyes widen, liking the swirling brown within their depths, reminding him of autumn.

'Yes, hassle. Hound. Harass. Call it what you like, but he wouldn't have wanted that.' Her words were short and sharp. Irritation made her breathing shallow and fast. Her breasts rose and fell rapidly beneath her T-shirt, snagging his attention as lustful hormones raced to places he just didn't need them going right now.

'He made me promise to bring you to Italy and involve you in the launch.' His words were sharper than he'd intended, but then he'd never expected to meet a woman who unleashed such a cocktail of fury and fire within him. She was not at all the sweet and happy girl Sebastian had told him about; she was sexy and passionately angry.

'He what?' She pushed the chair under the old pine table and moved closer to him.

Not a good idea, not when his body was reacting so wildly to her sexy curves. He wanted to drag the damn chair back out, keep the barrier between them. Maybe then he'd be able to think about the reason he'd come here instead of this long neglected need for a woman's body.

'The car is due to be launched. I want you there.' The words rushed out and he had the strangest sensation that she was depleting his control, weaving some kind of spell around him.

'You want me there?' Her voice raised an octave and he blinked hard, then realised how it had sounded to her. A little pang of conscience surged forwards but he pushed it back. Clearly she held him responsible for that night and he couldn't sully her memories with the truth. Not after the promise he'd made.

'Sebastian wanted you there.' What was the matter with him? This woman wasn't at all what he'd expected. She didn't look glamorous and the idea that she had, until recently, been living a luxury lifestyle didn't seem remotely possible.

Why did this ordinary and plain version of Charlotte Warrington, tousled and unkempt from the garden, arouse him so instantly? He couldn't process thought coherently, his body flooding with lust, demanding satisfaction.

She shook her head. 'No, he wouldn't have asked that. But then he wouldn't have been killed if it wasn't for you and your stupid car.'

'You know he lived for cars, for the thrill of speed. It was what he did, what he was good at.' Sandro pushed back the image of the accident, shelving the terror of all that had unfolded minutes after the crash, which had proved, within hours, to be fatal. He could relate to her pain, sympathise with her grief, but he couldn't and wouldn't allow her to apportion the blame to him.

He'd kept the truth from the world and the gossip-hungry media, out of respect for the young driver who'd quickly become his friend. Now it was time to carry out Seb's final request. He'd wanted his sister at the launch, wanted her stamp of approval on the car, and that was what Seb would have— whatever it took.

'It is also how he died.' Sadness deflated

her voice and he saw her shoulders drop. Was she going to cry? Panic sluiced over him.

As she composed herself, his gaze scanned the small country kitchen, typically English and not at all the sort of thing he'd imagined her living in. Herbs hung drying from a beam and various fresh versions adorned the windowsill. Nestled among them, in a small frame, was a photo of Sebastian and Charlie.

He reached for it and saw her gaze dart from him to the photo, but she said nothing as he picked it up and looked at the picture. Instead of being drawn to his friend, he looked at the image of the woman who now stood close to him. A woman he knew through the media but had never met. The same woman who was now having a strange effect on him—or was that just his conscience?

From the photo her eyes shone with happiness, her deliciously full lips spread into a smile. She was leaning against a sports car, her brother, his arms wrapped protectively around her, pulled her close, equally happy.

'Rome. Two years ago,' she said, her voice almost a whisper, and he sensed her move closer to him, felt the heat radiating from her body. 'Before he became embroiled in your project and forgot about us.'

He took a deep breath in, inhaling her

scent, something light and floral, like jasmine, mixed with an earthy scent from her time just spent in the garden. Carefully he replaced the photo on the windowsill, ignoring the barb of accusation in her last words. That was not a discussion for now. 'You are alike.'

'Were.'

That one word ratcheted up his guilt, the same guilt he'd told himself again and again he shouldn't carry and, finally, he'd thought he'd convinced himself. He should have known that coming here, facing this woman wouldn't be easy. That it would only increase the self-apportioned guilt instead of lessen it. The fact that he still kept Seb's darkest secret from everyone didn't help.

He looked down at her as she stood at his side and when she looked up, her mossy green eyes so sad, so vulnerable, his chest tightened, almost crushing him with a need to chase away that sadness, to put that happy smile back on her sexy lips once again.

'It's what he wanted, Charlotte,' he said softly, unable to break the eye contact.

'Charlie. Nobody calls me Charlotte. Except my mother,' she whispered. The kind of sexy whisper he was used to hearing from a woman after passionate sex. Inside his body, heady desire erupted as he imagined her lying in his bed, whispering with contentment.

'Charlie,' he repeated as wild need pumped through his veins. He really should stop his mind wandering to the subject of sex. He was in danger of complicating this mission beyond all proportions. She was the one woman he shouldn't want, couldn't desire. 'Seb did want you there.'

'I can't.' Her voice, still a throaty whisper, tugged at his male desires as they rampaged ever wilder.

'You can,' he said and, without thinking, he reached out and stroked the back of his fingers down her face. Her skin was soft and warm. Her breath hitched audibly and her eyes darkened in a message as old as time itself.

Slowly she shook her head in denial, moving her cheek against his fingers, and he clenched his jaw against the sensation, reminding himself he didn't mix business with pleasure and this had always been about business—and concealing his friend's downfall.

He thought again of the recent conversation with her father, of the assurances he'd made to him, binding him deeper into the promise Seb had extracted from him as his life had ebbed away.

'Your father thinks you should.'

It was as if an explosion had happened. As if a firework had gone off between them. She jumped back from him, the chair scratching the tiled floor noisily, her eyes flashing accusation at him.

'My father?' Her voice, laden with shock, crashed into his thoughts, bringing his mind well and truly back into focus. 'You've spoken to my father?'

Charlie was numb with shock. How dare he speak to her father? And why had her father not mentioned it? Why hadn't he warned her Alessandro Roselli, owner of one of Italy's biggest car manufacturers, was looking for her, wanting her to do something he knew she couldn't face yet? She'd only seen her father yesterday. He should have told her.

'What exactly have you spoken about with my father?' She kept her words firm, her fingers curled around the back of the chair as if the pine would anchor her, keep her thoughts focused and in control. Just moments ago she'd wondered what his kiss would be like, had revelled in the soft caress of his fingers like a star-struck teenager. What had she been thinking? 'You had no right.'

'I contacted him to ask if I could visit, to invite you to be at the launch. Your father knows it is what Seb wanted.' He folded his arms across his broad chest and leant against a kitchen unit, his eyes never breaking contact with hers.

For the second time that morning her shoulders sagged in defeat. She pressed her fingertips to her temples and closed her eyes briefly. Hopefully, when she opened them he wouldn't be watching so intently, so knowingly.

But it didn't make any difference. Those bronze-flecked eyes, which strangely felt so familiar, now bored into her. Right into the very heart of her, as if probing for every secret she'd ever hidden.

She dropped her hands and gripped onto the back of the chair again. 'You had no right to speak to my father. He doesn't need to be reminded of what we've lost and I'm more than capable of deciding for myself if I want to see you or not or if I want to be involved in the launch.'

'And do you?' He raised his brows and a smile twitched at the corners of his lips. The same lips she'd just imagined kissing her.

Did she what? Focus, Charlie. Her mind scrabbled to regain rational thought. She didn't know what she wanted except not to allow this man, this prime specimen of raw maleness, to know how unsure and undecided she was.

'I certainly didn't want to see you.' She raised her chin and injected calm control into her voice. 'If you recall, I asked you to leave. I don't want any part of the motor racing world any more.'

'Is that why you've hidden yourself away in the depths of the English countryside?'

The curiosity in his voice was barely disguised and the question came rapidly on the heels of the confusion he'd caused just by being here. She found it difficult to think about such things, but this man's presence was making it harder still.

'I withdrew from the frenzy of the media out of respect for my brother. I'm not hiding,' she said, aware of the curt tone of her voice. 'I couldn't continue to be on camera, promoting the team, not after Seb died.'

'Do you think he'd want you to stay that way?'

As he leant against the kitchen unit, unable to help herself, her gaze flickered to his hips and strong thighs. A sizzle of sexual awareness shimmied over her. Why did she have to find this man, of all men, so undeniably attractive?

'Meaning?'

'The cottage is very nice, but a woman like you shouldn't be ensconced here for ever.'

She looked back into his face, taking in the slant of his nose and the sensual curve of his lips. He looked directly into her eyes, almost knocking the breath from her body with the intensity.

Was he right? Would Seb want her to be involved? Then his last words finally registered in her mind. 'What do you mean—a woman like me?'

He walked around the table, appearing confined within the small kitchen. A room she'd never thought of as so compact, not until Alessandro Roselli had walked into it. He stopped at the opposite side of the table and she was thankful to have something more substantial between them.

'You live life in the fast lane—or did.' His accent had turned into a sexy drawl and his eyes raked over her. Again she was conscious of her casual and slightly grubby clothes.

'Well, now I don't and I have no intention of going back to it. Nothing you—or my father—can say will change my mind.'

'"Look after my little Charlie. She'd like you."' He spoke firmly and she knew exactly who he was quoting. Only Seb called her 'little Charlie'.

He pulled out another chair and sat down. He was taking root, making it very clear he wasn't leaving any time soon, but his words unsettled her. She could almost hear Seb saying them.

'I don't believe you.' She folded her arms across her chest, trying to deflect his scrutiny, but she remembered the phone calls from Seb. He'd always tried to get her to date again, insisting that not all men were as heartless as her former fiancé. 'He would never say that.'

Absently, he reached out and pulled last night's local paper towards him. He looked as if he belonged in her home, in her kitchen. He looked comfortable.

'It is true, *cara*.'

'Charlotte to you.' Her previous thoughts linked in too easily with his term of endearment and it unnerved her. She wished she'd never invited him to use 'Charlie'.

'Charlotte…' he said, so slowly, so sexily he caressed each syllable. Heat speared through her body. She stood rigid, trying to ignore the heavy pulse of desire scorching through her. What the heck was the matter with her?

Maybe she'd been out of the *fast lane*, as he'd called it, for too long. Should she believe him, that Seb had wanted her involved? Not that she'd ever admit it to him, but those words could well have been spoken by her brother.

'What exactly did my father say?' She had to divert his attention. She couldn't stand here any longer whilst his gaze ravished her. It was too unnerving.

He looked up at her, the paper forgotten, and the heat level within her rose higher still. She swallowed hard. Her brother had been right. She did like him, but purely on a primal level. It was just lust, nothing more. Something she would get over and she could do without that particular complication at the moment.

'He said,' he taunted her, his brows lifting a little too suggestively, 'that it was time you got back in the driving seat.'

His words hung heavy in the air. Words which were true. Hadn't her father said exactly that to her only a few weeks ago?

'I wasn't aware there was more to you than the glamorous façade you've always displayed on camera—that you'd been taught to drive high-powered cars.' He watched her intently and she had the distinct impression he was trying to irritate her, push her into accepting that her brother had wanted her to be involved.

She thought of her job promoting Seb's team, following them to every racetrack in the world and being interviewed by the press. It was a jet set lifestyle, one she'd enjoyed and had been good at. She'd got there by working her way up from the very bottom and had learnt all there was to know about cars and driving. Despite the glamorous image she portrayed to the world whilst on camera, she'd always felt safer, less exposed when she was doing what she really loved. Working on the cars and driving them—something her mother had been set against.

Was it time to stop hiding away and be part of that life again? She pondered the question, aware of his gaze on her, watching and taking in every move.

'You'd be surprised,' she flirted, shocking herself by doing so. What was she doing? She never flirted. It only ever caused trouble. She knew that better than most and had seen it many times in her line of work. Light-hearted flirting always led to more. Her mother had fallen victim to it, leaving her and Seb as teenagers whilst she pursued her latest love interest.

He raised a brow, his eyes sparking with sexy mischief, doing untold things to her pulse rate. It had to stop. She couldn't stand here any longer beneath his scrutiny. She'd melt.

'I hope I get to find out.' His voice was almost a drawl, making her stomach clench.

'Coffee?' Diversion tactics were certainly required and coffee was the first thing to come to her mind.

'Sì, grazie.' The effect she was having made him slip automatically into Italian. Coffee was the last thing he wanted. Even a good cup of espresso wouldn't distract him from the fire in his body.

She looked at him, her tongue sliding unconsciously over her lips, and he almost groaned with the effort of staying seated at the table when all he could do was watch her. Desiring a woman dressed in elegant evening wear was normal, but the way he wanted this casual and rumpled version of Charlie was totally new and unexpected. It was also extremely inconvenient.

He watched as she moved around the kitchen, taking in her curves as she turned her back to him to prepare the coffee. He liked the way her jeans clung to her thighs, accentuating the shape of her bottom. Her scruffy T-shirt couldn't quite hide the indent of her waist, just as it hadn't hidden the swell of her breasts from his hungry eyes moments ago.

She turned and passed over a mug of instant coffee, then sat at the table. Inwardly he grimaced. Not what he was used to, but if it meant he had time to convince her to at least be present at the launch then he would have to put up with it.

He took a sip, watching as she blew gently on hers, almost mesmerised by her lips. He had to rein in his libido. She was an attractive woman and in any other circumstances he would have wanted more—much more, at least long enough for the fire of lust to burn lower. But he had to remember she was Sebastian's sister and, out of respect for his friend's memory, she was off limits. He shouldn't have allowed his attraction to show, shouldn't have lit the fuse of attraction.

'Back to business,' he said tersely and put down his mug.

'I wasn't aware it was business,' she said lightly. A little too lightly, giving away that she was battling with emotions, that she was stalling him. 'I thought this was all about salving your conscience, freeing you of guilt.'

He did feel guilt over Seb's death—who wouldn't in the circumstances?—but it wasn't what drove him, what had made him come here. He'd come because of the promise he'd made. 'It is business, Charlotte. I want you to be at the launch of the car. Seb always wanted you there. He knew how good you were with the media.'

'He never said anything to me about being at the launch.' She put her mug down, pushing it away slightly, as if she too had no intention of drinking it.

He was about to say how much Seb had missed her. How he'd looked forward to her going to Italy. Anything to persuade her, when her next words jolted him with the raw pain entwined in them.

'But I suppose he didn't know he was going to die.'

He nodded, fighting his conscience and sensing she was coming to the right decision by herself. He just needed to give her a little more time. 'Sadly, that is true.'

'When is the launch?'

Her eyes, slightly misted with held-back tears, met his. Despite his earlier thoughts, he did feel guilt. Guilt for her sadness, and worse. He felt compelled to make it right, to bring happiness back to her life. After all, she wouldn't be hiding away from the world, the racing world in particular, if she wasn't unhappy.

'Friday.'

'But that's only two days away! Thanks for the advance warning.' Her tone was sharp and he saw a spark of determination in her eyes that he recognised and related to.

'*Bene*, you will be there?'

'Yes, I will,' she said as she pushed back her chair and stood up. Dismissing him, he realised. 'But on my terms.'

CHAPTER TWO

'WHAT TERMS?' ALESSANDRO asked suspiciously, looking up at her from where he'd remained sitting at the table.

Charlie watched his jaw clench and his eyes narrow slightly. He hadn't expected that. It annoyed her that he'd thought he could just turn up at the last moment and ask her to go to the launch of the car, as if she was merely an afterthought. Until now she hadn't wanted anything to do with the car, but she'd started to realise that by being involved she might be able to find answers to the questions she still had about the accident.

She mulled the idea over, trying to ignore his scrutiny. If—and that was a big if at the moment—she did go, she'd want much more than just being a last-minute guest. One invited only because Alessandro's conscience had been nudged. She'd want to know all there was to know about the car.

She regretted deeply that she hadn't seen Seb in the months before the accident. If she had gone to Italy to see the car as it had turned from dream into reality, would she have been able to prevent the fateful night of the accident?

The launch could be the exact catalyst she needed to regain control of her life. It was time to put the past to rest, but she could only do that if she had answers. This could be the only opportunity she'd get to find out what had really happened to her brother. He had been, after all, a professional driver, trained to the highest standard, and for Charlie his accident was shrouded in questions.

'Before we discuss my terms, I need to know what happened that night.' She folded her arms in a subconscious gesture of self-protection and leant against the kitchen cupboards, watching intently for his reaction.

She'd expected guilt to cloud his face, to darken the handsome features, but his steady gaze met hers and a flicker of doubt entered her mind. She'd always held him responsible, blamed him, but right now that notion was as unstable as a newborn foal.

'What do you want to know?' His calm voice conflicted with her pounding heart. The questions she'd wanted answers to since the night of the accident clamoured in her mind. The answers now tantalisingly close after having eluded her for so long.

'Why was he even in the car? It wasn't fit to be driven—at least that's what I heard.' She straightened her shoulders and took a deep breath, desperately trying to appear in control. She was far from that, and deep down she knew it wasn't just because she had to face the man she blamed. It was the man himself.

Alessandro Roselli's powerful aura of domination and control filled the kitchen, but she couldn't allow herself to be intimidated. She met it head-on, with determination and courage. She would find out the truth, one way or another. She was convinced it hadn't yet been revealed and she wanted to put that right.

He sat back in his seat, studying her, and she had the distinct impression he was stalling her in an attempt to divert her attention. It was almost working. She'd never been under such a hot spotlight before. *Think of Seb*, she reminded herself, not wanting to waste this opportunity.

'Do you always believe gossip?' He folded his arms, looking more relaxed than he had a right to. Far too self-assured.

She frowned, irritation at his attitude growing. 'No, of course I don't.'

'So if I tell you there was nothing wrong with the car, would you believe me?' He unfolded his arms and turned in his seat, stretching his long legs out, one arm leaning casually on the table. But he was far from casual. His body might be relaxed but, looking into those dark eyes, she knew he was all alertness. Like a hunting cat, lulling its quarry into a false sense of security. But not this mouse. No, she was on her guard.

Forcefully, she shook her head. 'The only thing that will convince me of that is to see the report of the accident.'

He stood up slowly, his height almost intimidating, walked towards the window and looked out across her garden and the countryside beyond. 'Would that really help? Every last detail is in it.'

'Yes,' she said and moved towards him, drawn by an inexplicable need to see his face, see the emotion in it. 'I want every last detail.'

'Why do you think your father hasn't shown you the report?' His broad shoulders became a barrier, as if he was hiding something, concealing something he didn't want her to know, like his guilt. 'What are you hoping to find?'

'The truth.' Anger surged through her again as she imagined him talking to her father, conspiring to hide all the details. She still couldn't understand why her father wouldn't tell her everything. She'd always suspected he was covering something up. Did he have loyalties to this man which exceeded those to his daughter—or even his son's memory?

He turned to face her, his expression hard, making the angles of his face more pronounced. 'Sometimes not knowing the truth is best.'

'What?' She pressed her fingertips to her temples, hardly able to believe what he was saying. Her father and this man were keeping things from her. He might as well have told her exactly that. 'What are you talking about?'

Alessandro heard the exasperation in her voice and gritted his teeth against the urge to tell her what she wanted to know. A truth that would tarnish all the happiness she'd ever shared with her brother and a truth her father had expressly asked him to conceal from her. That had been the one and only condition her father had made when he'd contacted him. He intended to honour that—and the promise he'd made to Seb.

She stood before him, not able to look at him as she pressed long fingers against her temples, her head shaking in denial. The rise and fall of her shoulders as her breath came hard and fast gave away the struggle she was having. Instinctively, he took hold of her arms and she looked back up at him, the beauty of her green eyes almost swaying him from his purpose. 'Your brother was in a high speed accident. You do know that, don't you?'

'I know,' she whispered, thankfully a little more calmly, and looked up into his face, her eyes searching his, looking for answers he couldn't give. 'But I need to know what happened and why.'

'It is better to remember him well and happy, believe me, Charlotte. It is for the best.' Her ragged sigh deflated all the anger from her body and he felt the resignation slip through her, defusing the fight which had raged moments ago.

'I know, but so many questions need answering.' She closed her eyes and he watched the thick dark lashes splay out over her pale skin. The urge to kiss her rushed at him, almost knocking the breath from his body.

When he'd arrived he'd never expected to find a woman he desired so fiercely. Only once before had such a need raged in him and he'd acted impulsively on it, marrying quickly, only to discover his wife had had ulterior motives all along. Under no circumstances would he put himself in such a position again.

The attraction which had sprung between him and Charlie the second their eyes had met complicated things, made his promise even harder to keep. He let her go and stepped back away from her, away from the temptation, curling his fingers into tight fists. The whole situation was testing far more than his ability to keep his promise.

She looked up at him, her chin lifting in determination. 'I will find out, Mr Roselli. Your and my father's insistence to keep things from me only makes it more important to do so.'

'Some things are best left alone. For Seb's sake, accept what you know and do as your father wants.' He moved away from her, back to the chair he'd sat in earlier—anything to put distance between them—but still the heady need which rushed through him persisted.

'For Seb's sake?' Her question jolted him and he realised how close he'd come to pointing her in the direction of the cause of the accident.

'Seb asked for you to be at the launch. It was one of the last things he said to me.' There was no way he was going to tell her Seb's actual last words and he guarded himself against letting the truth inadvertently slip. He held her partly accountable for Seb's problems. She'd never been to see him in Italy, had never shown any interest, but that wasn't something he was prepared to discuss now. All he wanted was for her to agree to be at the launch.

'He really said that?' Her voice was so soft it was hardly audible, but it did untold things to the pulse of desire he was fighting hard to suppress.

'He wanted you there.' He watched the indecision slide over her face and waited. She was coming to the right decision slowly. All he had to do was wait.

Charlie couldn't shake the feeling of unease. Yes, she knew Seb's accident would have caused horrible injuries, but she couldn't rid herself of the notion there was something else. Something her father wanted to keep from her as much as Alessandro did. Did that mean he was to blame?

She changed tactics and adopted an attitude of acceptance, realising it was possibly the only way to find out. Slowly, she walked back to the table and stood looking down at him where he calmly sat, watching her.

'If I come to the launch I want to know all about the car first. I want to see everything you and Seb worked on. I want to live it, to breathe it.' A hint of the passion she'd always felt for her job and the world of racing started to fizz in her veins after being unmoved for many months, infusing her with excitement that she hadn't felt for a long time.

'There isn't much time for that.' He sat back in the chair and looked up at her, observing every move she made until she wondered if he could read all her thoughts.

'If I'm going to be at the launch I want to be able to talk about the car, to bring it to life for everyone else. I need to know all there is to know.'

It was more than that, she admitted to herself. It was much more than just promoting the car. It was seeing what Seb had seen, feeling the excitement he'd felt as he'd driven it for the first time. Her thoughts halted as if they'd slammed into a brick wall.

Was she ready to know all the facts? She looked at the man she'd blamed for her brother's death. As far as she was concerned, he'd allowed Seb to drive a faulty car, despite the fact that her father had told her all the reports stated driver error. She'd blamed Alessandro and now he was here, offering her the opportunity to find out the truth for herself. Would he really do that if he had something to hide?

'I want to see all the files and every drawing Seb made.' She kept her voice firm, trying to hide the waver of confidence growing within her.

Alessandro got up and made his way around the table, coming closer to her, his face stern with contemplation. 'I can't allow it. There isn't enough time.'

Not allow it. Who did he think he was?

'If you knew anything about me, Mr Roselli, you'd know that I need to be involved—if I'm to do my job right, that is. You do want me to promote this car, put my seal of approval on it, do you not?'

She held his gaze, looked directly into his eyes. She would not be intimidated by him. He might be used to getting his way in business, but so was she. He pressed his lips together in thought, the movement drawing her attention briefly, but quickly she regained her focus, refusing to allow the pull of attraction to him to cloud her mind. Confirming her suspicions of his blame for the accident would surely curb any misguided attraction she was experiencing.

'It's more than that, isn't it, Charlotte?' The firmness of his tone dissipated as he said each word until he caressed her name, sending a hot fizzing sensation racing over her. It was worse than when he'd called her Charlie.

It was soft yet insanely hot, but she couldn't pay heed to that now. 'I need to know something about the car if I am to promote and endorse it. You understand that, surely.'

He took a deep breath in and she watched his broad chest expand, waiting expectantly, holding her own breath.

'I do but, given the circumstances, is it really wise?' He looked up at her and she tasted defeat as his dark eyes hardened in determination. But defeat wasn't on her agenda. She'd do this her way or not at all. How could he expect anything less when he'd been the one who'd let Seb get in the car, allowed him to drive it that night?

This was the only option. Her only chance to find out what had truly happened. At least then she might be able to move on from it. 'Don't worry—I won't dissolve into a heap of female hysteria again.'

'Maybe you should,' he said and stepped closer to her—too close—but she wouldn't move away. He must never know of the heat he fired within her, just from one look. Thankfully, he'd stopped his flirting of moments ago and had become more professional and she had to ensure it would stay that way.

'No, it is past time for that. I intend to do what my father advised last week.'

'And that is?'

'To get back in the driving seat.' She wouldn't tell him just yet that was quite literally what she intended to do.

He raised his hand to his chin, his thumb and finger rasping over the hint of dark stubble, the sound tying her stomach in knots. She couldn't listen to her body now, to the way it reacted just to being close to him, not that she really understood what it was asking of her. Heightened desire and intense awareness of a man was something she'd never experienced before.

Her previous relationships had been short-lived and unsuccessful. Back then, the breakdown of her parents' marriage had still been too fresh in her mind. Those relationships had also been a long time ago. The mess her parents had made of their marriage had ensured that lifelong commitment wasn't something she considered possible. There was no way she was going to expose herself to more hurt and humiliation.

'I'm not convinced it is for the best, but if you are sure then so be it.' He spoke slowly, his accent heavy, as he continued to watch her closely.

'I am,' she said quickly before he had a chance to change his mind. Before she too changed her mind.

'Then we have a deal.' He reached out his hand, the same one that had been thoughtfully touching his face, and she took it quickly, anxious to seal the deal.

'We have a deal.' Her words came out in a rush as a jolt shot up her arm, setting off sparks all over her body as if she'd become a firework. Her breathing almost stopped as his eyes locked with hers, his fingers clasped tightly around her hand, the warmth of his scorching hers.

'Bene,' he said firmly, so firmly it was obvious he didn't feel any of the drama from touching her and she'd do well to remember that the next time he smiled at her as if she was the most beautiful woman in the world. He was flirting, just like all the men she'd known, including her father. And it was flirting which had destroyed her parents' marriage, driving her mother into another man's arms, tearing the family apart.

She closed the door on those thoughts. Now was not the time to become embroiled in them, not when she had the perfect opportunity to find out the truth of Seb's last hours.

* * *

Alessandro held onto her hand and looked into her eyes. Did she feel it too? Was the same sizzle of passion creating havoc in her body? She regarded him with a steady gaze, her full lips pressed into a firm line. Evidently not. Her beautiful face was a mask of stone; not a trace of emotion there.

He should be pleased, grateful that the deal they'd just made wasn't going to be overcomplicated by sex. His friendship with Seb and the promise he'd made when he was in hospital, hooked up to all sorts of machines, dictated this arrangement should be business only. At least with her cool demeanour it would be exactly that.

'If it becomes too painful, too much, you must tell me.' She frowned at him and pulled her hand free of his, ceasing the torment just that innocent touch had created within him.

'It won't.' Those two words were so full of strength he didn't doubt it for one moment.

'You are very sure of that, considering you told me to leave only a short while ago.' Was he trying to reassure himself or her?

'You caught me off guard.' She reached past him and gathered up their discarded coffee mugs and as she turned to wash them he couldn't help but take another look at her curves, admire the womanly softness of them.

Enough.

Business. That was all it was—business. He also sensed that this was a woman who wouldn't accept a no-strings-attached affair. He had, after all, become adept at avoiding such women since extricating himself from a marriage which should never have happened.

He shrugged his shoulders, trying to shake off the pulse of passion. 'Then we shall travel to Milan today.'

'We?' Her eyes flew wide with shock.

'I have much to do ahead of the launch and if you seriously want to learn more about the car it would be a good idea, no?' He wondered at the wisdom of travelling with her when he found it hard to focus on much other than her glorious body.

'I'm not packed or anything. I'll travel out later. You'd better get back to your family.'

'That will not be necessary.' His voice was firm, perhaps a little too firm if the surprise on her face was anything to go by. 'There isn't anyone awaiting my arrival.' Those days were over and if he had any sense it would stay that way.

He didn't miss her raised brows, or the look of suppressed curiosity which crept into her eyes, and wanted to deflect any questions. 'There are also plans for the weekend, with customers going to the test track to drive the demonstration car. Seb had been really excited about that, told me you'd be in your element there.'

'But still,' she said, her soft voice torturing his unexpected need for her, 'I can make my own way there.'

Was she deliberately being difficult, provoking him to the point of frustration? 'I have a plane waiting. We can be there before nightfall.'

She looked at him, doubt clouding her eyes, and a vice-like grip clutched at his chest. Seb had always spoken very protectively of his sister—and now he knew why. She was woman enough to bring out the protective streak in any man. For years he'd avoided any such sentiments, having had them destroyed by divorce. He was far from the right man to protect her and he wished he'd never made Seb any promises.

He couldn't do this, couldn't risk it. She was sweet temptation even though he knew she was off limits. He couldn't do anything against Seb's memory. This was Seb's sister, the woman his friend had always wanted to protect. If he allowed this carnal need to take over, he would be failing in his promise to Seb. He wouldn't be protecting her at all.

'So what are you going to do while I pack?' Charlie asked tersely, annoyed that she hadn't even left her home yet and he was already making decisions for her. She tried for flippancy. 'Drink more coffee?'

'No,' he said, sounding very Italian, even with just that one word. 'I will wait here.'

He was infuriating and she recalled what Seb had said about him once when they'd talked on the phone about his new venture. *A man who knows what he wants and allows nothing to get in his way.*

Alessandro did want her at the launch. That much was clear. But why? Was she disrupting his plans by dictating her own terms? She certainly hoped so. It was probably about time he learnt he couldn't have it all.

'Very well. I will be as quick as I can.' She made to move past him and he stepped back away from her, giving her room. So much room that anyone would think he didn't want her near him, but the heavy hint of desire in his eyes gave an entirely different message.

'I'm not going anywhere, *cara*.' The silky softness of his voice stirred the throb of desire which still lingered inside her body. She clutched the door frame of the kitchen as if it was the only thing that would keep her upright.

'I wouldn't expect anything less from a man like you.' Before he even had time to respond, she fled, dashing up the stairs to her room, enjoying the rush of anticipation that ran through her. She paused briefly. She'd always been excited by the prospect of jetting off when she'd worked for Seb's team, but never had such a handsome man been part of the reason.

He's not, she scolded herself and quickly changed, before applying light make-up. Then, with practised speed and efficiency, she packed a small bag, just enough for a few days in Italy. She'd shop for anything else she needed once there.

His expression of shock made her smile as she returned to the kitchen. He hadn't expected that. At least it proved he didn't know as much about her as he claimed.

'Have you your passport?' His accent was heavy as he moved towards her to take her bag.

His fingers grazed hers as she gave him the bag and heat scorched her skin. She looked up at him and a flush crept over her face. In his eyes she thought she saw desire, the same desire she was sure must be shining from hers. Would he see it? Recognise it?

She hoped not. From the first second her eyes had met his, the pull of attraction had been strong. With each passing minute it had strengthened, but she could not and would not act on it. To do so would be disloyal to Seb. Whatever had happened the night of the accident, this was Seb's business partner.

She hesitated. Could she do this? Should she be considering going anywhere with this man? The desire he lit within her contrasted starkly with the anger she felt at her brother's death. As far as she was concerned, he was the reason her brother had crashed.

She'd do well to remember that.

This was going to be harder than he'd imagined. Sandro took the case from Charlie, taking in her change of clothes. Heels, tight jeans of soft beige with a white blouse and dark brown jacket. Chic. Elegant. Not at all like the dishevelled gardener he'd met on arrival. She was now very much the woman he'd seen on television promoting Seb's team. The woman he'd admired more and more as Seb had enthused about her.

Don't go there. He pushed thoughts of her to the back of his mind, focusing instead on maintaining a businesslike manner. One that would keep her where she needed to be in his mind.

He watched as she opened a drawer and pulled out her passport.

'I should really let my neighbour know I'm going away.'

He frowned, unsure where that comment was going. 'Why is this?'

'She'll keep an eye on the place, water the garden.' Absently she picked up her phone and began tapping quickly onto the screen. 'At least for a few days.'

Garden, he pondered. That didn't fit with the glamorous image she'd built up as she'd promoted the team. Had this cottage, this garden been her escape from the media frenzy that had followed? He knew well about the need to escape. It had been something he'd had to do twice in his life now.

'You gave up your career to become a gardener?'

She turned to face him, putting her phone in her handbag at the same time. 'Why is that so shocking?'

'Seb never mentioned you were a gardener.'

'It is something I've always enjoyed, but I didn't feel the need to change my life before Seb's accident.' She looked up at him, her expression serious and focused. 'Seb's death changed all that. That's why I want to know all he did that day. I have to understand why it happened.'

Each word echoed with her accusation, leaving him in no doubt she blamed him. The only other person who knew the truth was her father—and he'd insisted that she must never know all the details of Seb's accident.

Thoughts of Seb grounded him and the urge to tell her everything, just to clear his name of blame in her eyes, was overwhelming. But he wasn't doing this for himself; he was doing it for Seb. He would do well to remember that when he next thought of succumbing to the temptation of Charlie. She was out of his reach. Put there by his sense of honour and his promise to Seb and subsequently her father. Out of his reach was where she had to stay.

CHAPTER THREE

As DARKNESS BEGAN to descend the car pulled
to a halt outside Alessandro's offices and
Charlie got her first view of the place she'd
heard so much about from her brother. His
calls had always been full of excitement and
pride as he'd enthused about the Roselli fac-
tory, workshops and test track.

Sadness crept over her too. This was where
Seb had spent his final weeks and she could
have been part of that if she'd accepted his
offer to come out and visit instead of being so
tied up in her career. The same career she'd
dropped after Seb's death.

She got out of the car and stood looking up
at the buildings, wishing she had come to see
what he was doing. 'I should have come when
he asked me to,' she said softly and was startled when Alessandro responded.

'Seb always hoped you'd come here one
day.' His voice was gentle and not at all judge-

mental as he placed his hand in the small of her back. She drew in a ragged breath, her emotions all over the place. Memories of Seb mixed with the undeniable attraction she felt for Alessandro. Guilt added to the mix and washed over her. How could she even be thinking such thoughts? Quickly she blocked them out.

'I wish I had.' Her voice was a croaky whisper of raw emotion. She stood next to him in the warm evening air, her emotions exposed and vulnerable, as if she stood before him totally naked. She was certain that not only was he able to see every bit of her skin, but into her heart and soul.

He stopped outside a glass door and keyed in his pass code, his other hand sliding away from her back, the heat of his touch cooling, giving her space to think. Judging by the shiver which had run up her spine, she needed that space. Badly.

'Why didn't you?' he asked, pushing open the door, stepping inside and holding the door open for her, but she didn't miss the lightly veiled accusation in his voice.

'It was busy. You know how the end of the racing season gets.' She saw his jaw tighten, saw the sceptical look on his face and shame heated her cheeks. She'd also been worried about Seb's blatant attempts at matchmaking. He'd often teased her on the phone about finding the perfect man for her.

She could have come. She'd wanted to come, but she had been a tiny bit threatened by this new life Seb had found. They'd always been so close and when he'd met Alessandro all that had changed overnight. She was pleased he'd found something he was so passionate about; she'd just never expected it to take him so far away from her, physically or emotionally.

He shrugged nonchalantly but she knew what he was thinking. She could almost hear his words, heavy and accented, telling her she was selfish, and she retaliated as if he'd actually spoken. 'I didn't know time was against me.'

He let the door go and she stood in the semi-darkness of the large reception. His face was a mask of hardened fury as the accusation in her words hit him. Did he feel any guilt? Did he have regrets? Did he want to go back and change things?

He stepped forward, coming closer, and she wished there was more light, something to lessen the presence of a man who excited and angered her so intensely. She veered wildly between those two emotions as he looked directly at her.

'Whatever guilt you carry, Charlotte, I do not need it added to what I feel.' His voice had deepened, become growly, anger lingering dangerously beneath the surface like a serpent waiting to strike. He loomed over her in the dim light, every bit the predator, but she wasn't going to be his next victim.

'Just by saying that you are admitting guilt.' She rounded on him. The hours spent on the plane and in his car, when she'd thought everything through silently, had allowed her temper to brew and now it flared to life.

For a moment his gaze held hers, his eyes hard and glittering. Tension stretched almost to breaking point between them as silence settled after her angry words. In her head she could hear her heartbeat, the fast thump of blood rushing around her body. It should have been ignited by her anger, but the flutter in her stomach as he stepped closer made it something else entirely.

It was raw attraction. Something she didn't want to feel. Not now and not for this man.

He stepped even closer, his height towering over her in the darkness, and she looked up into his eyes, wanting to appear fearless but afraid he'd see just what an effect he could have on her. Could he hear her heart pounding? Had he noticed her breath, ragged and unsteady?

'Dangerous words, *cara*.' Each word was low and soft like a cat purring, but she sensed the coil of tension in him, the cool detachment from the emotions that careered inside her. He was more like a tiger preparing to strike.

'I came here to see what Seb had been working on,' she said, trying hard to beat down the flutter of emotions, and walked away from him towards the stairs. 'So, can we just do that? Then I'd like to check into a nearby hotel.'

She didn't wait for his answer, didn't look at his face, but every nerve in her body told her he was watching her—intently. She was about to go up the stairs when light flooded the reception area and she blinked against it and turned to face him. The sleek clean lines of the interior of the building were exactly as she would have imagined and, unable to help herself, she looked around her, trying hard to ignore the man who stood in the centre of the marble floor and the superiority which radiated from him.

'This way,' he said and passed her as she waited at the foot of the stairs, his scent of musk and male trailing in his wake. 'We'll take the lift.'

She bit her bottom lip, anxiety rushing at her. Was she really ready to see what Seb had been working on? She wasn't, but this was what she had to do, what she needed to do before she could put the last year behind her.

She became aware that Alessandro was watching her, waiting for her to enter the lift. 'We don't have to do this tonight.'

Was that genuine concern in his voice? Her gaze locked with his and everything around them spun. Everything blurred as the dark depths of his eyes met and held hers. Time seemed to be suspended, as if everything was standing still. She lowered her lashes. Now was not the time to get fanciful. She'd never been that way inclined, had never hankered after notions of instant attraction. So why now? And why this man?

'I want to.' The words rushed from her as she stepped quickly into the lift. 'I just hadn't anticipated it. Today started just like any other, then you arrived…' Her voice trailed off and she looked down at her hands, feigning interest in her unpainted nails.

'I should have contacted you first but I didn't think you'd see me.' His tone was calm and so matter-of-fact she glanced up at him.

He appeared totally unaffected by the whole situation.

'I wouldn't have.' She flashed him a smile and, from the expression on his face, he hadn't missed the sarcasm. 'I wouldn't have seen you and I would never have come here.'

The lift doors opened onto a vast office but she paid little attention to the hard masculine lines and marched out of the lift, drawn inexplicably to the wall of windows, offering an unrivalled view of Milan's twinkling skyline.

She should feel too irritated by his assured presence to notice even one thing about his office, but that was so far from the truth it was scary. She should be thinking of Seb, should be focusing on what he'd done here, not the man he'd worked with.

'*Grazie.*' The deep tone of his voice unsettled her and, as she stopped to look out over the city, she saw his reflection behind her, saw him move closer.

'What for?' Her gaze met his reflected in the glass and a coil of tension pressed down inside her. She knew at any minute it could snap.

'Your honesty. Saying you wouldn't want to see me.' His reflection shrugged nonchalantly, his gaze so intense it obliterated the view. All she could see was him. Then her heart plummeted in disappointment. None of this really mattered to him. It was all about the Roselli image and launching a new car.

'I have no reason to conceal my dislike of you, Mr Roselli.'

Liar! a voice called in her head. She didn't dislike him. She should. The fizz of attraction was at war with the blame she still laid at his door, despite his earlier assurances that the accident had been nothing more than a tragedy.

'Dislike. Is that not a bit strong?' He moved unbearably close, his eyes holding hers in the reflection in the window.

She had to stop this now, whatever *this* was. Something she couldn't control was happening between them and she didn't like it. Or did she?

'Oh, I dislike you intensely, Alessandro.' She turned, her words a hurried whisper. Who was she trying to convince? 'And right at this moment I have no idea what I'm doing here.'

His eyes turned blacker than the night sky, their swirling depths mesmerising. She couldn't break eye contact. The power he'd had as he'd looked at her reflection had been intense, but this all-consuming fire which had leapt to life in her was too much.

'You are here, *cara*, because you couldn't help yourself.' His voice was deep and gentle, caressing every heightened nerve in her body into submission. 'Because this is what you need to do—for Seb.'

At the mention of her brother's name the spell slipped away like morning mist as the sun came up. She could see everything sharply and in focus again. She was here for Seb—a fact she had to keep in the forefront of her mind—or lose it to the seductive charms of the worst man she could possibly fall for.

'Exactly.' Her eyes maintained contact with his and she saw the moment they turned to glittering blackness. 'So I'd like to see where he worked, what he did.'

Alessandro couldn't move, mesmerised by the intensity of what had just passed between them. For the last few weeks he'd been irritated at the thought of contacting Seb's sister, had put the moment off for as long as possible. But, whatever he had been expecting when they'd finally met, it wasn't the raw desire that coursed wildly through him.

If she'd been any other woman he'd have acted upon that need; he would have kissed her and explored the passion that lingered expectantly, just waiting for the touch-paper to be lit so it could explode into life.

'*Si, così,*' he instructed her to follow, unable to gather his thoughts quickly enough to use English, a situation he'd never known before.

'Thank you.' Those two words were so soft, so seductive he almost couldn't move. He fought the urge to press his lips to hers. Thankfully, she stepped back, enough to remind him what he should and definitely shouldn't be doing.

With intent, he made his way across the vast expanse of his office, resisting the urge to look in the windows and see her reflection following. He didn't need to. His body told him she was; even if he hadn't heard her footsteps on the marble behind him he would have known she was there.

'This is where Seb worked.' He went through a door at the end of his office into the room Seb had claimed as his own, the emptiness of it almost too harsh. On the far wall was the first drawing that Seb had done of the car. But still the office looked stark.

Something akin to guilt touched him. He should have brought Charlie here sooner and not left it until the last days before the launch. He should have done this a long time ago, but he'd been anxious to conceal the truth—for Seb's sake as much as his sister's.

As Charlie walked past him he caught a hint

of her perfume; instantly he was transported back to her garden and the sweet smells of an English summer. Her deep ragged breath, inhaled quickly, drew his attention back to the present.

'Is this what he did?' She stood next to the desk, her fingertips tracing the outline of the car drawing. He noticed her hand shook slightly and, when she looked back at him, hesitation weaved with panic sprang from her eyes. He had the strange sensation his heart was being crushed.

'*Sì.*' His voice was so raw he couldn't say anything else, painfully aware he was intruding on her moment of grief.

'What else?' She looked at him and he saw the gleam of tears collect in her eyes and the pressure on his chest intensified.

Thankful for the diversion, he walked over to the desk and opened the laptop, turned it on and looked across the desk at her. Her pretty face was pale, her eyes wide, reminding him of a startled doe. 'There are lots of photos on here, as well as all he created in the design programme.'

She hesitated for a moment and he wondered if it was all too much. She stood and watched him as he opened the photos up on the screen and turned the laptop to face her.

He felt her scrutiny and questions press down on him.

Slowly she reached out, one fingertip touching the screen. He watched her eyes, the green becoming much more intense as she looked at the photo of Seb sitting in the driving seat of the test car, and he inwardly cursed. Couldn't he have selected a more appropriate photo for her to see first?

'When was this taken?' Her voice was fragile as she continued to look at the screen. She swallowed hard, trying to keep the tears at bay, and for the first time ever he wished a woman would cry. She needed to let out her grief.

He hated the answer he was going to have to give. 'The day before the accident.' It took huge effort to keep his voice calm, to keep it steady, but even to his ears each word he'd just said sounded cold. He'd studied the photo since then, shocked to see a hint of trouble in Seb's eyes. Would she notice too?

She looked up at him and tears filled her eyes, making them shine like gemstones. Before he'd thought about the consequences, he moved around the desk and took her in his arms. Without hesitation, she sought the comfort he offered and pressed her face in her hands, her forehead on his chest as sobs racked her body.

'*Dio mio*. This is too much for you.' He wanted to clench his fists in anger but instead spread them over her back as the sobs continued, smoothing them over her and pulling her closer against him.

'No, it's not.' The strangled words came out in a rush, muffled by her hands and his body.

'It is, *cara*, it is,' he soothed, just as he'd done for his sister many times as they'd grown up, but this wasn't his sister. This was a woman he desired with every nerve in his body.

'I should, I should.' Sobs prevented her words from coming out and, without thinking, he lowered his head, pressing his lips into her hair. She stilled in his arms momentarily and he closed his eyes against the memories of when he'd thought his life was complete. He pushed back the knowledge that he'd failed to be the man his wife had wanted, lifted his chin and took in a deep breath.

It seemed like for ever that he held Charlie as she cried, each sob transferring her pain to him, increasing his guilt for not having been there the night Seb had decided to take the car out again. He would have seen the drink- and drugs-induced euphoria and could have stopped him. The discovery still shocked him now. How had they worked so closely together for all those months without him noticing Seb had such a problem?

He lowered his head, once more pressing his lips against her hair, his aim to soothe both of them. But, as he held her tighter, uttering words of comfort in Italian, he knew he had to stop, had to let her go. It shocked him to admit he wanted to be more than just a shoulder to cry on.

Thankfully the tears subsided and a huge sob shuddered through her. She looked up at him and they were so close they could have been lovers. Without any effort at all he would be able to press his lips to hers, but her tear-stained cheeks reminded him they were not lovers and exactly why they were here.

'I should have done this a long time ago.' Finally she spoke a little more calmly, her words slightly wobbly after crying.

'This is the first time you have cried?' Incredulity made him pull back slightly as he watched her expression change, become softer, less pained.

She smiled up at him, nodding. 'Thank you.' Her voice was barely above a whisper and she blinked as tears escaped her eyes. She rubbed one cheek roughly with her fingers but, before she could reach the other cheek and before he could think about what he was doing, he gently wiped the tears away.

Everything changed in that second. They became cocooned in a bubble of sizzling tension. Unable to stop himself, he held her face in his hands, her skin warm and damp from crying. Her green eyes locked with his, sadness and grief swirling with something quite different and completely inappropriate.

'Prego.' His natural response sprang to his lips but his voice was husky and deep. He couldn't take his gaze from hers, couldn't break that tenuous contact which held them together.

She closed her eyes and leant her cheek against his hand. Instinct took over and he caressed her face then pushed his fingers into her hair, the silky softness of it almost irresistible. He wanted to kiss her, to lower his head and taste the fullness of her lips.

He moved towards her and she opened her eyes. For what seemed like an eternity she looked up at him, her breathing fast and shallow. His heartbeat sounded so loud in his ears as he watched the green of her eyes change until they swirled with browns, like trees as autumn approached.

He wanted her. That was all he could think of at that moment. Nothing else was important. Nothing else mattered.

She moved nearer, her eyes closing, spreading her long damp lashes on her cheeks, and then her lips met his. It was a gentle kiss, full of hesitancy at first, but, as he pulled her close, one hand buried in her long hair, it deepened, became something much more. He shouldn't be doing this, not now, not ever.

Charlie's head spun and she knew she shouldn't be kissing him like this, knew it would only mean complications, but the need to feel his lips against hers was overwhelming. Her senses were on overdrive, every nerve in her body responding to him. Heat exploded deep inside her and she pressed herself against him. His arm tightened around her back, pulling her closer, and his fingers scrunched in her hair, holding her head at just the right angle as his tongue moved between her lips, entwining with hers.

Her arms slipped up around his neck, pulling him closer, deepening the kiss until she could hardly stand, her knees were so weak. Never had a kiss felt like this, so electrifying, so right.

With a force and suddenness that nearly

knocked her backwards he released his hold on her and pushed his hands against her shoulders, forcing her back and away from him. She was so shocked she didn't know what to say, even if her laboured breathing had allowed her to speak. After a few seconds he let go of her, stepping backwards, a wary look in his eyes and a furious rush of Italian sprang from his lips.

Her grasp on the language was slight and she had no idea what he'd said, but his body language left her in no doubt. He had not enjoyed or wanted that kiss. So why had he encouraged her? Was this some kind of game?

'That shouldn't have happened.' She forced herself to stand as tall as possible, even though her knees were so weak they might crumple beneath her and a fire of heady need still raged inside her.

'Damn right it shouldn't have.' He flung his hand up in agitation, turned and marched across the office to the doorway. 'That can never happen between us, ever.'

Hurt scolded her but she kept her eyes firmly fixed on him, refusing to be intimidated. He didn't want her kisses—so what? 'I didn't think…' she stammered the words out '…I didn't know what I was doing.'

His eyes narrowed but he remained at the

far side of the office. 'Apparently not. It's time we left here.'

'No—' she panicked, her embarrassment at his obvious dislike of her evaporating '—I haven't seen nearly enough.'

'Enough for tonight.' His voice was deep and hard, the complete opposite to the husky tones that had soothed her just moments before. 'You will stay with me tonight.'

'You?' The question shot from her lips before she could think.

'You are upset, acting irrationally. I cannot leave you in a hotel alone, not tonight.'

The firm words brooked no argument and if she was honest she had little fight left in her. The last twelve hours had been nothing short of shock after shock. From the moment he'd arrived in her garden she'd been on a roller coaster ride of emotions.

'Just call me a taxi to take me to a hotel in the city.' With bravado she was far from feeling, she walked towards him but he didn't move aside for her to leave the office. Instead, he looked at her, his brown eyes cold and remote.

'Seb was right.' The firmness of his voice caught her attention and she looked up at him, her gaze locking with his.

Angered at the mention of her brother,

she glared at him. 'And what is that supposed to mean?'

A hint of a smile lingered at the edges of his mouth then he pressed them into a tight line of exasperation. 'I know more about you than you might think, Charlotte Warrington.'

'You've got a nerve,' she said as her own expression mirrored his.

'*Sì.*' He shrugged casually and turned away from her, leaving her wide-eyed with shock.

If she was sensible she'd just walk out of here, get a taxi to the airport and go home. But right now she wasn't sensible and she wanted this chance to get answers to questions that would otherwise niggle at her for the rest of her life.

The only problem was these answers were tied up with the man she blamed for Seb's death, the very same man she'd just thrown herself at, kissing him with a passion she'd never known before.

'I'm not going anywhere with you, especially after what just happened.'

He turned round so swiftly she almost walked straight into him, leaving her perilously close to him again. 'Do I need to remind you, *cara*, you kissed me?'

Her cheeks burned as the sexy depth of his voice practically caressed her body, reigniting the heat that had flared between them earlier. 'That,' she hissed at him, 'was a big mistake. One that won't be happening again.'

'Va bene!' His gaze searched her face, resting briefly on her lips. 'In that case, there is no danger in you staying at my apartment tonight.'

'Danger? You make me sound like some sort of predatory female.' She was becoming more and more infuriated by him. Maybe a hotel would be the best option, but as that thought settled in her mind she knew she didn't want to be alone right now. Not after all she'd been through in the short space of time since he'd forged into her life, but her only choice of company was Alessandro Roselli.

He just quirked his brows at her, the humiliating spark in his eyes clear. She held his gaze, refusing to back down.

'Why do you want to do this? Why is it so important I'm at the launch?' She gestured around the room, glancing back at the drawing on the wall.

'As I explained, I made a promise to your brother. One I intend to keep.' He walked through to the large office they'd entered earlier and across to the lift. 'This way, *cara.*'

Charlie couldn't shake off the feeling that he'd won. What he'd won she didn't quite know, but he had. One night in his apartment wouldn't be that hard, would it? First thing, she'd arrange a hotel in Milan and as soon as the launch was over she could go back to her cottage and get on with her life. The quiet life she'd led since Seb's accident; the one that kept her safe.

Alessandro shut the door of his apartment and watched Charlie as she walked into the open-plan living area. She hadn't said a word since they'd left his office but, despite that, the tension between them had increased. So much that he now questioned his sanity in bringing her here.

'The guest suite is ready for you,' he said sternly, eager to create some boundaries because if there was one woman who needed to be behind them it was this one.

'Thank you,' she said so softly it was almost a whisper.

He watched her as she walked around the apartment, judging the artwork he'd collected over recent years, taking in just about every detail with a hint of suspicion on her face. There was nothing modern about the apartment, from the grand façade of the old building to the ornate interior. It was a complete contrast to the office they'd just left—exactly what he'd wanted it to be. It was a showcase for the real Alessandro.

She wandered over to the balcony doors and looked down onto the busy streets of Milan. He used that time to rein in the hot lust which pumped around his body after the journey back from his office. Since the moment her lips had touched his something had changed and he feared it might be irreversible.

'Would you like anything to eat or drink?' The polite question gave him just that bit more time to regain control and bring normality to the evening.

She turned and looked back at him. 'No, thank you. I'm tired. It's been an unexpectedly busy day and I need to be fresh tomorrow.'

'Fresh?' The word sprang from him, a frown furrowing his brow, but she kept her gaze on him.

'Yes, there is a lot to do before the launch, lots I need to know.' She looked completely focused but the gritty determination in her voice rang alarm bells in his head.

'You're right,' he said and turned from her, picking up her small overnight bag before heading towards the guest suite. A good night's sleep would be beneficial to him too, but somehow he doubted he'd get it. His body still craved hers, still yearned for her touch, her kiss.

He crunched his hand tightly around the handle of the bag. He'd made a promise to Seb and he would keep that promise, no matter what. The thought of his friend, who had also been a partner in the business venture, reminded him that Seb had been the last person to stay in the guest suite.

He pushed aside the guilt. Seb had been staying with him. He should have seen the signs, spotted the problem. He couldn't change that now, but he could keep the painful truth from Seb's beloved sister.

He paused outside the door and turned to look at her. 'Your brother stayed here too. Did you know that?'

'No.' A startled whisper formed the word and she looked at him, confusion marring the beauty of her face. 'I don't understand. He was looking for somewhere to rent.'

'That is true.' He opened the door to the suite and walked in and she followed him, looking around her. There wasn't any evidence that anyone had ever stayed here. 'It was a sensible option. We were both working on the same project.'

'Did he find somewhere to move to, or was this the last place he stayed?'

The very question he'd dreaded had just been delivered with clear words. 'This was the last place.'

'But his things?'

'I sent them on to your father.'

She looked around the room, from the large bed to the dark wardrobe and drawers, as if she didn't quite believe him. 'I see.'

Silence floated down around them, a silence so heavy he wanted to break it, to say something. But what else could he say? Everything so far had caused hurt and pain. 'There is another room. Much smaller, but if you would prefer it…'

She shook her head, the light above them catching the darkness of her hair, making the brown tones glow and come alive. 'I'd like to stay here, please.'

Now he really did question his sanity. Not only had he kissed her, responded to the invitation her lips had made, but now he'd put her in the very same room Seb had last stayed in. The promise he'd made to his friend to look after Charlie, to involve her in the project was becoming more difficult to keep by the minute. As was concealing the truth.

CHAPTER FOUR

'DID YOU SLEEP WELL?' Alessandro's polite enquiry pulled Charlie from her thoughts as they sat having breakfast together in the tranquillity of his apartment. The jeans and shirt he wore hugged his body to perfection and she fought hard to keep her mind where it should be—on her brother and the car she was here to help promote. Thinking about the handsome Italian she'd kissed last night wasn't going to help her at all and she forced herself to be as rational and in control as he appeared.

'Yes, thanks,' she replied, taking a sip of freshly squeezed orange juice. Sleeping in the room Seb had used should have helped her, but it hadn't. It had had the opposite effect. She'd wept silent tears for her brother, finally finding release from the grief she'd kept locked away, but little comfort. It hadn't banished the idea that Alessandro was to blame for the accident or that he was hiding something from her.

He looked at her, his keen gaze lingering on her face just a little too long. She was aware the dark circles beneath her eyes would tell him she hadn't slept well at all. Thankfully, he had the good grace to let it go.

'There are a few things I need to do this afternoon in preparation for the launch, but we can either go to the office or to the test track this morning.'

Test track. Those words careered into her, dragging her back to a time when she'd always been at the test track, her father and brother at her side. It was where she'd learnt to drive, really drive, much to her mother's disgust.

'I'd like to see the car,' she said thoughtfully. 'It feels as if I haven't been at a track for a long time.' She'd missed the thrill and excitement of the place. Her garden, whilst a safe sanctuary she'd been happy in, suddenly seemed tame.

'*Sì,*' he said as he sat forward, placing his now empty cup back on the table. 'Seb told me it was a big part of your childhood too.'

She looked into her juice, not able to meet the intensity in his eyes. They made her feel vulnerable and she didn't do vulnerable. 'I spent a lot of my time there. I loved it.'

'What did your mother think of that?' His question nudged at issues which had erupted often when she was a teenager.

'She didn't have any objection to Seb being there.' Charlie hesitated and looked up into his handsome face and instantly wished she hadn't.

He appeared relaxed as he sat back in his seat again, but something wasn't quite right. He reminded her of a big cat, lulling its quarry into a false sense of security. Any moment he would pounce, strike out and get exactly what he wanted with unnerving accuracy.

'I sense a *but*.' He spoke softly, then waited, the silence hanging expectantly between them.

Before she could think, his question had thrown open things she'd do better to keep to herself—because it was a very big *but*. How much had Seb told him? Did he know of her mother's disapproval of her involvement in the racing world? Did he know she'd hated the lifestyle, hated the way her husband had flirted with all the women. Her mother had resented being second best so much she'd left the family home, deserting her teenage children.

'My mother didn't like me being there. She didn't think I should be driving those cars and certainly not working on them. She thought I should behave more like a lady instead of a tomboy and it became a constant battleground as I grew up.' She wasn't bitter any more. In fact she could now see why her mother had been so against the racing world, why she'd wanted her daughter as far away from it as possible. But she wasn't about to go into all that now, especially not with Alessandro.

He smiled, a gorgeous smile that made his eyes sparkle, full of mischief. 'Now I understand. Your insistence on being called Charlie was to remain a tomboy.'

'Something like that.' She finished her juice, wondering how she had become the topic of conversation.

'But you are a beautiful woman, Charlotte, why hide it?' The intensity in his eyes scared her, made her heart pound, and she bit down on her lower lip, suddenly very much out of her depth.

'I was a rebellious teenager,' she explained, giving in to the need to offer some sort of explanation. Heat infused her cheeks and she looked out over Milan to hide her embarrassment. It was time to change the subject; she'd said more than enough to him. This wasn't about her—it was about Seb. 'Can we go now? I'd like to see the car.'

'Of course,' he said as he stood up, preparing to leave. 'If you are sure this is what you want to do.'

She'd never been more certain about anything, which was strange, given that just twenty-four hours ago she'd thought she never wanted to see this man. His timing had been impeccable, arriving so soon after the conversation she'd had with her father about getting her life back again.

'Before we go,' she asked, unable to keep the hint of suspicion from her voice, 'what did my father say to you when you told him about the launch?'

He looked directly at her, his stance bold and intimidating. 'It appears he wants only your happiness.'

'I need to contact him, tell him I will be at the launch.'

'He knows.' She looked at him. There was not a hint of conceit on his handsome face, but she sensed he was keeping something from her. She decided to let it go—for now. At the moment, seeing the car which had become Seb's world was at the top of her list and talking like this wouldn't help at all. She tried to deflect his interest with light-hearted words.

'And will he be there too?'

'He hopes to be.'

'That sounds like Dad.'

'This way,' he said as he picked up his keys and slipped on a leather jacket. The understated style only emphasised the latent strength of his body and she had to pull her gaze away, force herself to think of other things. This was not the time or the place to become attracted to a man—especially not this man.

Alessandro wasn't able to negotiate the morning traffic of Milan with his usual ease. He could hardly concentrate on driving. His main focus was instead on the woman beside him. She didn't say anything, merely looked around her, taking in the vibrancy of the city he loved.

'Have you always lived in Milan?' Her voice was soft and should have soothed his restless mind, but it didn't. The slight husky tone to it only intensified the way his body seemed on high alert just being next to her.

'For most of my adult life, yes.' He knew it was only small talk, but discussing his family with outsiders wasn't what he usually did. But Seb had become like a brother to him, even in such a short time, so didn't that make Charlie anything but an outsider?

'Seb mentioned your family lives in Tuscany and produce wines.' Her voice was light in an attempt to make conversation, but such questions made him uneasy. When a woman asked about family, there was usually intent behind it. But what motivation could Charlie possibly have?

He shrugged and turned onto the open road, leaving the city behind as they headed for the test track. The sun shone with the promise of another hot day. 'That is true, but my love was for cars, not wine. So I moved to Milan, finished my education and began working for my uncle, turning the company around and making it the success it is today. The rest, I believe you would say, is history.'

'And this car? Was that also part of your love for cars?' She almost caressed the words, setting his pulse racing at an alarming rate.

He glanced across at her, watching as she looked around the interior with genuine interest, proving all that Seb had told him about her was true. She wasn't much older than his sister but, at twenty-four, had made her way to the top of her career, promoting first her father's racing team, then Seb's. She was a successful woman in her own right, and that success had been born out of her passion for cars and racing, which was why Seb had wanted her at the launch of the car.

She ran the tips of her fingers across the dashboard in front of her, leaving him in no doubt of her love of cars—and that she was a woman of passion. She'd shown him that much last night with her kiss. He pressed down on the accelerator in a bid to focus his attention on anything else but her, and the car responding willingly. Thinking of last night's kiss wouldn't help to quell the lingering desire she'd awakened.

'Impressive,' she said quickly, laughter filling her voice.

Inwardly he groaned. She thought he was putting the car through its paces for her, when all he'd been doing was giving his mind something other than her to focus on. Again he glanced at her, shocked to see a smile on her lips, and instantly he wished he wasn't driving, that he didn't have to concentrate on the car so that he could enjoy her smile—the first real smile he'd seen on those sweet lips.

'It is not far now.' *Grazie a Dio!* He didn't think he could take much more of this enforced proximity, the way her light perfume weaved its scent throughout the car. His body was excruciatingly aware of each tiny movement she made.

The streamlined car willingly ate up the miles as they drove in a silence laced with tension—not angry tension but that of restrained desire. Her kiss last night had more than hinted at her attraction for him. He couldn't deny that he was tempted by her but it was something he wouldn't act on. To do so would be to dishonour his friend's memory and the promise he'd made.

A sigh of relief left him as they turned off the road and down a smaller road which led to the Roselli test track. Never before had a drive here been so long and so tense. Thankfully, he parked the car behind the large building which housed the prototypes for all his cars currently being tested.

Charlie got out of the car, her full attention now on the building before her, and he knew she was anxious. The tight set of her shoulders betrayed her nerves. 'You don't have to do this. We can just go back to the office.'

She turned to look at him, her hand reaching up to keep her hair from her face as the wind toyed with it. Instantly he remembered how he'd pushed his hands through it just hours ago, how he'd clutched it hard to enable him to kiss her deeper, and the way she'd responded.

Maledizione! Did he have to keep going

back to something that should never have happened?

'Mr Roselli, I want to do this and I will, no matter how many times you try to dissuade me.' The fire of her spirit sounded in every word and, as she looked at him, her pretty face set in fierce determination, he fought the urge to smile.

'I think we can dispense with formalities now, don't you, Charlie?' He saw her green eyes glitter as he used her preferred name.

'As you wish, Alessandro.' The sweetness of her voice didn't mask her irritation.

'Sandro,' he said as he locked the car and came round to her. 'I'd much prefer it if you'd call me Sandro.'

Her gaze locked with his, challenging him with unsaid words. They held the same fire and courage Seb's always had, although the green of hers was more like emerald. Hard and glittering.

'As you wish, Sandro.' She shrugged casually and turned to look up at the building. 'Now, can I see the car?'

'It is only the test car. The actual car will be revealed at the launch.'

She glanced briefly at him before returning her attention to the modern building, its streamlined design which curved around them. 'Even better. I'd like to know what changes have been made since Seb drove it.'

There it was again. Accusation.

'It is an exact copy of the prototype Seb drove. There weren't any improvements to be made.'

She turned and looked at him, her brows raised in surprise. 'None at all?'

He watched her intently for a moment as she did anything other than look at him. 'No. This way.' He moved purposefully towards the door, keyed in his code and stood back for her to enter, hoping she wouldn't pursue the conversation further. He didn't want to lie to her, but at the same time he didn't think she would be able to handle the truth.

His team of mechanics were working on another project and glanced up as they entered. He noticed she ignored their speculative gazes and instead walked towards the grey test car parked in the centre of the white workshop floor, ready for them.

He followed but held back as she approached the vehicle, wanting to give her time with something that had been as much a part of Seb's life as it was his.

She paced slowly along the car, her long jeans-clad legs doing untold things to him, and he gritted his teeth against the sizzle of attraction. This was one woman he couldn't have but, as she slid her hand over the front wing of the car, following the sleek angles of the bodywork, he couldn't help but wish he was the car.

'Can I?' She gestured towards the door and he nodded, not able to string even a few words together in any language after those thoughts.

As she slid into the driving seat he moved towards the car and leant on the open door. He looked down at her, trying hard not to notice how the seat curved around her thighs. Instead, he kept his eyes on her face, watching as she openly devoured everything with hungry eyes. Slowly she wrapped her fingers around the steering wheel, clutching it tight until the leather creaked. She looked as if she belonged behind the wheel of a car and as if this particular car had been made for her.

'It's amazing.' Those words were so light and husky. He gritted his teeth hard, trying to subdue the lust which now throbbed in his veins, demanding satisfaction.

With a sudden movement which caught her attention, he pushed his body off the car door. 'We'll take it out now,' he said as he gave the signal to his team to raise the doors. Sunlight poured in as they silently opened.

'I'd like to drive.' Her words were firm as

he walked back to the car, reminding him of the stubborn little girl he'd grown up with. His sister had nearly always got her way with such a tone, especially with him.

'Maybe it would be better if I drove first.' He didn't want her thinking too much about her brother whilst behind the wheel. It was obvious she blamed him for Seb's accident and grief could manifest itself in various forms. 'You can sit back and enjoy the ride, just as Seb would have wanted you to.'

'You didn't know Seb that well if you think that.' She raised her delicate brows suggestively at him and smiled. He knew he was beaten. 'Seb would want me to drive so he could sit there and listen. He'd want to feel the car and be at one with it.'

He leant on the car, one hand on the roof, one hand on the open door, and lowered his head, bringing him very close to her. The enticing scent of her perfume met him and he resisted the urge to inhale it. Her passionate little speech just now had already done enough.

'*Va bene*, you may drive, but carefully and I will, of course, be with you.'

She smiled up at him, a genuine heartfelt smile that made her eyes light up. Right there and then he decided he wanted her to smile more and assigned himself the mission of making that happen.

'I am able to drive.' Her lips formed a sexy little pout as she put on a show of pretend petulance and it was all he could do not to lean down and kiss her. The first woman who'd stirred his dormant body since he'd extricated himself from the mistake of his marriage and she was out of bounds. So far off limits she might as well be on the moon.

'I don't doubt that you can, but having dealt with one female who drove too fast I'm reluctant to do it again.'

'Oh.' The word was full of disappointment and he couldn't hide his smile.

'My sister. A while ago now. She took a corner too fast, despite my warnings, and ended up a bit the worse for wear.' He made light of it when really he wished he could go back and change things, make her listen. Just as he now wished he could with Seb.

'Well, you don't need to worry about me,' she said and started the engine, the throaty growl forcing her to raise her voice slightly. 'Sebastian Warrington was my brother, after all.'

She was wrong, so wrong. He did have to worry. His promise to Seb meant that not only would he involve her in the launch but he'd look after her, be a brother figure to her, and he couldn't do that when hot lust shot around his body like off-course fireworks.

He walked around the front of the car, watching her through the windscreen. Her face was full of concentration as she studied the array of information on the driver's screen. As if she sensed his scrutiny, she looked up and smiled, this time a more hesitant smile. Should he be letting her do this? He knew only too well what could happen if someone drove beyond their capabilities.

Her gaze followed him as he moved to the other side of the car and opened the passenger door. 'Ready?' He kept the word light as he slipped down into the seat and shut the door. It was a lightness he didn't feel, not when they were suddenly very close, much more so than in his car.

She nodded her head and looked forward, focusing on the task, but he couldn't concentrate. The engine growled in anticipation and the car moved slowly out into the morning sunshine. He breathed a sigh of relief that she wasn't as hot-headed as her brother had been the first time he'd taken it out.

Carefully she manoeuvred out onto the track and with a steady speed began the first circuit. He looked over at her, taking the opportunity to study her as she focused on driving. Her thick hair was scrunched up in a haphazard sort of style, looking as if she'd just left her lover's bed. Her lips were pressed together in concentration, the same gesture Seb had used when he really focused on driving, but on Charlie it was cute, sexy even.

The engine grew louder as she pushed the speed up, bringing his mind back from the dangerous territory it had just wandered to.

'Relax.' The laughter in her voice didn't match the intense concentration on her face and, probably for the first time ever, he didn't know what to say. With shock, he realised she was making him nervous. He sensed she was holding back, that, just like her brother, she wanted to take the car to its upper limits, but was she capable? Could she really drive a car like this to its full potential?

'You're not nervous, are you?' The teasing question finally focused his mind. 'I have been taught to do this properly.'

'No,' he lied as he tried to sit back and relax. With each passing second it was obvious she could drive and if she'd had the same tutor as Seb, what more guarantee did he need? 'I make a bad co-pilot. I like to be in control at all times.'

She glanced quickly at him, the green of

her eyes flashing with amusement. 'Are we just talking about driving?'

He couldn't help the laugh that rumbled from him. 'I was only referring to driving, but now you come to mention it…'

'Let's see what she's made of then.' The laughter in her voice gave way to a serious tone full of purpose.

Before he could utter one word of protest, the car lurched forward like an angry stallion, pressing him back in the seat. The trees around the track blurred as the engine roared. His heart pounded and he had images of arriving at the scene of his sister Francesca's accident and comforting her while he waited for help to arrive.

'Slow down!' he demanded, hating the sense of being totally unable to avert a crisis.

'Don't spoil it now. I know what I'm doing.' Her raised voice did little to assuage the doubt he had in himself to trust her driving ability.

'Charlotte!' He snapped her name loudly, keeping his eyes firmly fixed on the corner they were hurtling towards.

Charlie could barely hear Alessandro. Her heart was thudding with the excitement of being behind the wheel of a powerful car again. It had been too long and she had no

intention of stopping now. This was exactly
what she needed to chase the demons away.

She pressed harder on the accelerator,
elated to find the powerful engine still had
more to give. As the countryside blurred to
a sway of green she knew this was the right
thing to do. Seb had driven this car, felt its
power and had been at one with it. Driving it
now brought her closer to him; it was as if he
was here with her.

'Slow down, Charlotte. Now.' Alessandro's
curt tone was full of authority but she couldn't
stop now, couldn't deny herself this moment.

'This is amazing,' she enthused, pushing
the car to its limits around a corner. Tyres
squealed but held the track like nothing she'd
known before.

'Do you ever do as you are told?' The rich
timbre of his voice was edged with steely control. She sensed him sitting there, rigid with
anger at her disobedience. The thought made
her laugh.

'Didn't Seb tell you that I'm exasperating?'
Another corner took her concentration and
beside her he cursed fluidly in Italian. Was
she really worrying him or was it just that she
wouldn't do what he wanted? There wasn't
any doubt in her mind that he was the type of

man who liked to be in total control of every situation.

'That, *cara*, is something we didn't discuss. Slow down.' His voice was firm, full of discipline, making her smile and itch to push the car harder.

'Do you always spoil everyone's fun?' She slowed the car enough to be able to talk with him, but the engine protested, tempting her with its power once more.

'Only when my life is on the line.' The acerbic tone of his voice didn't go unnoticed as he raised it to be heard over the engine. They headed down a long straight and she had to resist the urge to push the car harder.

'Your life is not on the line, Sandro—don't be so dramatic. I've been trained to the highest level to drive cars just as powerful as this.' She drove into the next bend, restraining herself from showing him just how capable she was of handling the car.

'By whom?' Those two words were curt and heavily accented and she wondered again if he genuinely was afraid.

'My father. He taught Seb and me everything he'd learnt, so relax and enjoy your car, feel it, be at one with it.'

She pushed the car into another bend, her body infused with adrenaline, something she'd missed when she'd taken up the more genteel pursuit of gardening. It just hadn't given her the same buzz.

A long straight stretch spread out before her again as she came out of another bend and, forgetting everything, including the hurt and pain of losing Seb, she pushed the car to its limits one last time.

It felt so good. Nothing like it on earth had ever come close. It was exhilarating. The car ate up the tarmac as they sped along the straight stretch.

'*Dio mio*, stop!' The harsh command penetrated the bubble of excitement she'd slipped into and she let her foot off the accelerator, the car slowing.

'We're halfway around the track; I can't just stop!' she protested, but moderated the speed to a more sensible level.

'Stop. Right now.'

'Right now?' Anger sizzled inside her. Anger because she had to do as he told her. Anger because she'd lost control in front of him but, most of all, anger at him. If things had been different, it might have been Seb at her side.

'Now, Charlotte.' His hard tone brooked no argument.

'Okay, have it your way.' As the words

snapped from her she pressed hard on the brake pedal.

Tyres squealed in protest as the front of the car lowered dramatically to the tarmac, but it was nothing compared to the anger which still hurtled around her. This was all his fault.

'Are you insane?' The car jolted to a stop and those words rushed at her.

She couldn't look at him yet. Her heart thumped so wildly in her chest she was sure he could hear its wild beat. She was mad, yes, she'd lost control. In her bid to forget the real reason she was here she'd been reckless, but it was still his fault.

'Yes—' she turned her head sharply to look at him, her breathing coming hard and fast '—I was mad to come here with you.'

Before she could think in any kind of rational way, she threw open the door, unclipped the seat belt and bolted—from him and the car. She ran from everything she'd tried to hide from these last twelve months.

'Charlotte!' She heard the deep tone of his voice, now edged with exasperation, but she didn't turn, didn't stop. She marched off the tarmac and onto the grass without any idea of which way to go. All she wanted was to get away from him, away from the car and away from all the pain which now surged through her.

Pain he'd induced.

As she began to break into a run he reached her, grabbed her arm and pulled her so quickly to a stop that she was turned and jolted against the hardness of his chest. For an instant all the breath seemed to leave her body and she couldn't speak. All she could do was stand looking into his eyes, glittering with anger as he held her captive with his firm grip. Her breathing was now so rapid she was panting as if she'd just run a hundred-metre sprint.

'Let me go.' Her furious demand only made his hand tighten on her arm.

'Not until you calm down.' He said the words slowly, but she didn't miss the glinting edge of steel within them.

'It shouldn't have been you.' A cocktail of emotions rushed to find expression. 'I should have been here with Seb. Not you.'

'I should never have brought you here, not after what your father told me.' Each word was delivered in a cool and calm tone, but there was still that underlying steel.

'My father?' She gasped in shock, trying unsuccessfully to release her arm from his grip. 'What has he said?'

'That you've been hiding from this since

the funeral.' He released her arm but remained excruciatingly close. It was all becoming too much. Memories of Seb entwined with whatever it was between her and this man. She couldn't deal with either of them at the moment.

'I have not been hiding from anything— except the cruelty of the media.' She looked up into his face, so close she could smell his aftershave, but fury kept her expression hard.

He blinked, his head drawing back from her just a fraction. 'The media?'

She pulled free from him, turned and stalked away, tossing her next words over her shoulder. 'Yes, the media. You know the ones. They like to dig all the dirt on you and your family when you're down.'

'Charlotte, don't walk away from me.' His tone was harsh but she carried on walking— or was she running yet again?

'Just leave me, Alessandro. Take the car back and leave me.' She stopped and turned to look at him; his strides were so long that he was almost directly behind her and again she found herself against a wall of pure maleness.

'No, *cara*.' He spoke more softly, looking down at her.

Infuriated, a well of exasperation opened deep within her. 'Worried what everyone will think when you go back alone?' She couldn't prevent the tart edge creeping into her words.

'I don't give a damn about anyone else. The only thing that matters right now is you.'

She looked up into his eyes; the angry glitter was gone from them now. She resisted the urge to close hers, to give in to the invitation of his words and let him care for her, soothe her. But that hadn't been what he'd meant.

'Why? Because of your promise to Seb?' she retorted, fighting back once more.

His brow furrowed and he shook his head in denial. Guilt niggled at her. She was deliberately provoking him. *It's his fault Seb isn't here*, she reminded herself sharply.

'Not completely.' He stepped closer, so close she could just reach up and kiss him if she wanted to. Just as she'd done last night.

Mesmerised by his nearness, the heady scent of his aftershave doing strange things to her senses, she remained exactly where she was. Their eyes locked and she was sure he was thinking the same thing, feeling the same hot sizzle arcing between them.

Slowly, maintaining eye contact, she raised her chin up and saw his eyes darken to the blackness of a starless sky. She paused, an unspoken question emanating from her. His answer was to claim her lips with his.

CHAPTER FIVE

CHARLIE CLOSED HER eyes as every limb in her body weakened beneath the power of his hungry kiss. Just when she thought she wouldn't be able to stand any longer his arms wrapped around her, pulling her so tight against him that she was in no doubt he wanted her.

What was she doing? Kissing this man—and, worse again, wanting so much more?

Although she knew she shouldn't, she couldn't help herself and, just as she had done the previous night, she wound her arms about his neck, sliding her fingers into the curls he had tried to disguise.

Adrenaline from the drive still pumped around her, fuelling this new heady passion to heights she'd never before experienced. Every part of her was on fire, burning with desire for the man she supposedly hated above all others.

'This is…' she began as his lips left hers,

scorching a trail down her throat until she couldn't utter another word.

'Amazing, no?' His husky voice sent a thrill of shivers through her.

No, not amazing. It's wrong. It shouldn't be happening.

Inside her head the words formed, but that was where they stayed as he claimed her lips once more, so deeply and passionately she gasped in pleasure against him. She couldn't think any more. The only thing that mattered was satisfying the hot need which blazed inside her.

'And this…' He almost groaned the words out as he lowered his head to kiss down her throat. She arched her back, leaning against the strength of his arm, knowing exactly what he wanted.

A sigh of total contentment slipped from her and she let her head drop back as his kisses moved down her throat until he reached the soft swell of her breasts, visible at the opening of her blouse.

Then passion exploded as he kissed her nipple, dampening the silk of her blouse. Her bra offered little defence against the persuasion of his seduction and she buried her fingers into the thickness of his hair, a soft sigh escaping her lips as she surrendered to the pleasure of his mastery.

'This is good too, no?' His accent became heavier with each word as desire engulfed them, wrapping them up together. He nipped at the hard peak of her nipple, sending a spark of urgent need straight to the very core of her.

'It's so good, but so wrong.' Her voice was a throaty whisper as she pushed her fingers deeper into the curls, pressing him against her, even though she knew it was reckless. Each breath she took intensified the sensation until she couldn't do anything but close her eyes to the pure pleasure of the moment. Wrong or right, she gave herself up to it.

'Oh, *cara*, it's wrong, so, so wrong, but so right.' He moved his attention to her other breast and she almost sank to the grass beneath her feet as his tongue worked its magic, her breathing ragged and fast.

'We shouldn't.' Barely a whisper now, her voice sounded hoarse as each breath rushed from her.

It was so good she thought she could hear horns—car horns blasting around them, their fast rhythm matching the pulse of desire inside her. The sound became louder and suddenly he straightened, pulling her upright with a jolt.

'*Maledizione.* I should have known we'd be seen.'

The sound of horns was very clear now and she realised it wasn't just horns, but emergency sirens. She jumped back from him as if scalded by his very touch, wanting to put as much distance between them as possible while she fought to regain control over her body, extinguish the heady need he'd ignited. Thankfully, he seemed to want the same and walked abruptly away.

What had she been thinking? Nothing. Absolutely nothing. That was the problem. She hadn't been thinking at all. She'd allowed her seesawing emotions to get the better of her and when she next spoke to her father she'd find out just what he and Alessandro had discussed. Had her father tried to continue the matchmaking Seb had started?

Alessandro took in deep breaths, trying to cool the heat in his body as he strode back to the track. The approaching ambulance was almost upon them as he reached the car. He didn't look back at her, but knew she'd started to follow him. Every nerve in his body responded to each step those lovely long legs took.

After a few quick words with the ambulance crew he sent them back to the workshop, by which time Charlie was at his side. What would have happened if they hadn't been interrupted? The thought of what he could at this minute be doing sent his pulse sky-high.

'Get in.' The command was gruff, but that was the only way to deal with this. Denial wasn't usually his style, but right now it suited perfectly. He got into the driving seat and waited, his gaze firmly fixed ahead as she got in beside him.

'Sorry.' That one word from her was so soft, so quiet he wondered if he'd imagined it.

What was she sorry for? Driving like a maniac or setting light to the fire between them? Either way, he didn't want her apology. He just wanted to get as far away from her as possible so that he could reassemble the barrier he always kept around him.

He didn't ever want to be so emotionally exposed with a woman, but Charlie had slipped under his radar, almost destroying the defence he'd erected after his marriage. It had taken just one kiss.

'I can't believe you'd drive like that. What would Seb say?' He clutched at the first thing that came to mind to use as a weapon against the hum of desire threatening to rise once more, just from being close to her. He could still smell her scent, still taste her and his body craved more, wanting absolute satisfaction.

'Seb would be pleased. He taught me to drive like that but, judging by your reaction, I guess he didn't tell you that I am a test driver for the team. I can drive as fast and as safely as any racing driver.'

'That may be so, but he wouldn't have wanted you to risk your life.' Angrily, he rebuffed her explanation.

A heavy silence filled the car and he wished the words unsaid. When she didn't say anything else he started the car and gently moved off, keeping the speed to a sensible level.

'Did I scare you?' The question flew out and he gripped the steering wheel, the muscles of his forearms flexing.

She had scared him, but he wasn't about to admit that to anyone. As the speed had increased all he'd been able to think of was Seb, lying in the hospital bed in pain, and the way he'd forced him into a promise he now had serious doubts he could keep. How could he look after Charlie as if she were his sister when all he could think of was taking her to his bed?

'Yes, damn it, you scared me. You knew I had to deal with my sister after she'd had an accident.' He wasn't about to confide in her the real cause of his fear. That would mean looking deeper at what had just happened between them. Accepting that there even was something there, some undeniable attraction that was so powerful it took over, given the slightest opportunity.

'I don't see how me driving on a test track has any connection with your sister having a bump on the road.' He could hear the irritation in every word and was relieved to see the workshop coming into view.

'That *bump*, as you put it, caused her to defer her last year at university and all because she couldn't slow down, as I'd asked her to do.' His mind began to tie in knots, talking on one subject, trying to rationalise another and fighting the need to pull over and finish what he'd started back there.

He'd never been this off-kilter before. Shock and the unrelenting need to regain control had unbalanced his emotions, but he couldn't let her know that.

'What happened?' Curiosity filled her voice and it was all he could do not to look at her. The heat of her gaze burned into him.

He drove back into the workshop, switching the engine off. Silence settled around them and he looked about the workshop, thankful

the mechanics had had the presence of mind
to make themselves scarce. He'd have some
smart talking to do with them later; of that
he was sure.

He threw his hands up in frustration. 'She
drove too fast. That's it. Just as you did out
there.'

He didn't need this conversation right now.
It wasn't what they should be discussing, even
though it went part way towards his reasons
for demanding she stop.

He could feel her watching him and turned
to look at her, instilling as much control as he
possibly could into his voice. 'She took a bend
too fast, hit the wall and ended up in hospital.
All because she couldn't slow down.'

'But I'm a skilled driver; I test drive for
Seb's team.' Her expression served only to
exasperate him further. Couldn't she see the
similarities between her and Seb? He was a
skilled driver too and now he was dead.

'Skill isn't everything, *cara*. Seb was incredibly skilled.' Her eyes widened and he
had the strangest sensation that he'd walked
into a trap. One of his own making.

'Seb went out in a car that should never
have been on the test track. Is that what you
are saying?' The accusation was hurled at him,
but he knew it was the driver that shouldn't

have been out on the track that night. If he hadn't been meeting with potential customers, maybe he would have seen the state Seb was in. Stopped him from taking the car out to the test track.

'Nobody knew he was here, Charlotte. He took it upon himself to take the car out.' He desperately tried to instil patience into each word. She was hurting and this was the moment he'd been dreading, the moment she'd accuse him of negligence and he wouldn't be able to deny it. Not if he kept the horrible truth from her.

'I thought he was staying with you. Surely you knew he'd gone to the test track?' Her eyes narrowed and he knew for certain she blamed him.

'He was staying with me, but he also did his own thing. I thought he was on a date that night.'

'And you just happened to be at the track within minutes of the accident.'

'Am I on trial here?'

'By me, yes.'

'*Va bene.* For the record, I was on my way back from a meeting and called in to collect paperwork. I wanted to go over the problem we had with the first prototype. The second had just come out of the workshop so I wanted to talk to Seb about it.'

Her face watched his expectantly and he wondered if she'd already heard this from her father, or read about it in the press. It had been a tough few months after the accident and he'd had to deal with the guilt he felt, even though no blame had been apportioned to him or his company.

'But Seb was out in the car?' she asked, pre-empting him.

'I'd seen Seb's car outside when I parked, but thought he'd gone out with one of the mechanics. When I noticed the test car gone, I knew he was out in it and jumped into the pickup. That's how I was able to be there just minutes after it happened.'

He could still hear the sickening thud and scrunch of metal, then the protest of the engine before the ominous silence. He'd known instantly it wasn't going to be good and was on his phone, calling for the emergency services as he'd pulled up alongside the twisted wreck.

'Thank you,' she whispered, her gaze lowering so that her thick long lashes brushed against her cheeks and he had to fight hard not to reach out to hold her or offer her comfort. He just didn't trust himself, he wanted her so fiercely.

'Come, that is enough for today. I'll take you back to the apartment.'

A little sigh escaped her as she got out of the car and, without a backward glance at it, walked towards the door. Quickly he caught up with her and as soon as they were outside the workshop he put his arm around her shoulders in an attempt to console her.

'Don't.' She pulled away from him and stood by the passenger door of his car, looking anywhere else but at him and very much like she was hurting.

Damn it. He should never have responded to her kiss last night and certainly shouldn't have done what he had today. Now he couldn't offer her comfort, couldn't keep his promise to Seb and look after her—like a brother. How could he go back from that intensely heated moment they'd shared at the trackside?

The drive back to the apartment had seemed to last for ever, but Charlie kept up the act of hurt and betrayal. It was hard, but more preferable to the role of wanton seductress that she'd just played out with him at the trackside. She was completely shocked by her behaviour. She'd never thrown herself with such abandon at a man and couldn't understand what had possessed her to do that today—other than hot lust. All she wanted now was to lie on her bed and be alone, to calm her body and her heart.

'I have work at the office this afternoon.' His words were firm but she knew he was looking for a way out, trying to avoid a discussion about what had happened between them. Well, that suited her just fine. She didn't want to acknowledge it either, much less discuss it.

'I may go shopping,' she said, trying to sound light and carefree. 'I need something to wear at the launch tomorrow evening.'

'I will send a car for you in a few hours. Rest first.' He stood tall and proud in the middle of his living room, the opulence of it still not quite fitting with the picture of the man Seb had painted in her mind.

Rest. She wasn't sure she could, but she was glad that at least she'd be alone. His gesture of comfort had been hard to shrug off earlier. She wanted nothing more than to be held by him, to be safe in his arms, but she didn't trust herself. Whatever it was between them, she could only ignore it if she physically kept her distance.

'Alessandro?'

'Yes.' He looked at her, his dark eyes no

longer full of the passion she'd seen in them at the test track. Now they were cold, full of dismissal.

'Your sister? Is she all right now?'

'Yes, thankfully, she made a quick recovery and even graduated with full honours.'

She nodded, unable to say anything, the pain of losing Seb more raw than it had ever been. She wished she could allow Alessandro to hold her. She'd never felt so alone. 'But Seb didn't.'

Without another thought, she went to him, needing his strong embrace and the warmth of his body. He didn't say a word as he took her in his arms, infusing her with his strength, but it felt different. Every muscle in his body was tense.

She pulled away. She shouldn't have done that, not after this morning.

'I won't be back tonight,' he said curtly, picking up his car keys.

She blinked in shock. Was she driving him out of his own home? 'Because of me?' Her voice was hardly a whisper and she bit her bottom lip with her teeth.

'Not you—me.' The sternness in his voice didn't go unnoticed. 'I think it's for the best. Boundaries have been crossed, but it won't happen again.'

She stepped back further from him. 'Good, but you don't have to stay away on my account.'

'I do, Charlie, I do need to—for Seb and the promise I made him to look after you.'

'You are looking after me.' She really should let him go, simply because she didn't trust herself not to want him. His offer to leave her alone became more tempting by the second as her heart hammered harder while he stood before her.

'My staff will see to your every need and a car will be available to take you wherever you need to go. I will see you at the launch.'

'Not before?' Stunned, she couldn't believe it. The launch was the next evening. Was he going to keep as far from her as possible for the next twenty-four hours? Did the boundaries they'd crossed mean that much?

Alessandro stood and looked at her, wanting nothing more than to take her back into his arms, hold her and inhale her sweet scent. But he couldn't. It would be disastrous if he did. He'd already proved she was the one woman who made him lose his mind and he knew if he stayed there would be no stopping him.

'No, it will be better if I don't.' He kept his voice level and stood rigidly straight, but didn't miss the look of disappointment slide across her face.

'But this is your home.' Her delicate brows furrowed in confusion and concern.

'Tonight it is yours. I will go elsewhere.' He had to. He already knew beyond doubt that he had very little self-control where she was concerned. He didn't want to be involved with any woman, but especially this one.

'To a friend?' She dropped her gaze and he knew exactly what she thought. That he was going to warm the bed of another woman. Well, so much the better if it stamped out the electricity that raged between them and the heady lust he felt for her. One thing was for certain; it couldn't go on, not if he wanted to honour his promise to Seb and keep his sanity.

'Something like that, *sì*.' He moved towards the door, needing to go before he relented and told her he was intending to spend the night in his office, something he did on occasion. His office was all geared up for such nights, but this would be the first time he'd been driven there by a woman.

It certainly wouldn't be as hard as staying here with Charlie when all he wanted was to make her completely his. But she could never be that to him, not now.

'*Buonanotte, cara.* Sleep well.'

CHAPTER SIX

IT WAS ALMOST twenty-four hours since Alessandro had left her at his apartment. Charlie had enjoyed the indulgence of being alone to begin with. She'd spent the first hours in her room, the same room Seb had stayed in, looking for anything left behind that connected with him. Any clues as to what he'd been doing in the days before the accident, but that had proved futile. She realised it was foolish to think there would be any evidence left in the room a year after he'd last been here. So she'd turned her attention to the rest of the apartment to learn about the man who owned it.

Old and new blended tastefully with the ornate interior of the grand building and she still couldn't help but be shocked that he didn't live in a new and modern apartment with the same masculine lines as his office. She wondered which was the real man—the one who worked in the modern minimalist office or the contented man who surrounded himself with fine art.

Now, she stood looking out over Milan as she waited for the car to take her to the launch party, unable to comprehend how much she was looking forward to seeing Alessandro again. A brief call from him, which had sent a sizzle of anticipation down her spine, had informed her he would send his car at six. As an ornate clock struck the hour she began to have second thoughts about the long red dress she'd bought that morning.

Second thoughts were too late. The car pulled up and her breath hitched as Alessandro got out. From her vantage point at the window above him she could see that he now wore a tuxedo and looked more sexy and stunning than any man had a right to. She drank him in. He looked like every woman's dream, the strength of his body still evident despite the high-class tailoring.

She watched as he shut the car door, grateful she had time to get her wayward thoughts reined in. She saw the black fabric stretch across his broad shoulders as he leant down and spoke to the driver. Unable to tear her eyes away, she stood watching, enjoying her unobserved vantage point.

As if he sensed her presence, he looked up at her. Despite the three floors that separated them, his gaze met hers, sending her pulse rate into freefall. If he could do this from that distance, what was it going to be like when she was actually with him?

She didn't have to wait long to find out as the key turned in the lock of the front door and he walked into the apartment, overpowering the splendour of the living room completely.

He stood and looked at her very slowly, his gaze moving down from her head to her toes, peeping out of the red sandals that gave her a few inches more height. Defiantly she looked at him, desperate not to let him know that inside she was melting from the heat of his gaze.

'Sei bellissimo.' He moved towards her, each step making her heart pound harder. His Italian was more sexy than his accented English. Her heart soared. He thought she was beautiful.

Shyness swept over her and she lowered her gaze. The vibrant red dress she had bought in a moment of defiance was having more of an effect than she'd imagined possible. She'd been drawn to the red sequins which sparkled on the bodice, and the jaunty single shoulder which had slashed red across her pale skin.

But now she wondered and looked down at the silk of the floor-length dress. 'It is not too much, is it?'

'Too much,' he said in a husky tone as he stepped closer and lifted her chin with his fingers, forcing her to look into his handsome face. 'You look beautiful.'

'Thank you.' She shyly accepted his compliment and stepped back, away from temptation. All she could think of was kissing him again, feeling his arms pressing her against his hard body. But she couldn't; she had to remain aloof, keep him at a distance. He'd already proved what he was capable of doing to her. 'I'm glad you approve.'

He didn't say anything. He didn't have to; the intensity in his dark eyes told her he more than approved. His gaze was so hot she could hardly breathe and she caught her bottom lip between her teeth.

'We had better go.' A ripple of awareness cascaded through her as his deep, sensual voice left her in no doubt that he wanted to kiss her, that he too was fighting an attraction so strong the outcome now seemed inevitable.

'Yes.' Aware how husky her voice had become, she moved quickly towards the door, the silk of her dress moulding to her legs as she moved. He followed her, his shoes beating a purposeful rhythm on the marble floor.

Whatever it was that had simmered between them that first afternoon in her garden had ignited spectacularly, threatening to engulf them at any second. She drew in a deep breath as she realised she wanted the increasing desire to burn freely between them. After several years of pushing men away, using her off-camera tomboy image to discourage male attention, this was what she now wanted. Was it just lust or was she ready to risk her heart again?

He shut the door of his apartment with a resounding bang which echoed in the coolness of the marble hallway, startling her and knocking all those tempting thoughts out of her mind. She turned to face him. 'Is something wrong?'

Purposefully, he walked towards her, stopping so close she could smell the heady scent of his aftershave, feel his breath on her face. She looked up at him and swallowed hard against the urge to kiss him.

'This is wrong.' The deep tones of his voice were heavy with accent and raw with unquenched desire. The sheer potency of his sexual magnetism made any kind of reply impossible. All she could do was look into his increasingly black eyes.

He lowered his head and brushed his lips over hers, the kiss so light her lips tingled. She sighed in pleasure, swaying towards him. She wanted him and whatever she said, however much she denied it, her body would call to his. Could something so potent be so wrong? Did she have to give her heart to taste the desire between them?

'So, so wrong, *mia cara*.' His lips left hers fractionally as he spoke, his voice husky with the same passion which flowed around her body. Her stomach churned nervously as her body heated in response to his desire-laden words.

'How can it be wrong?' She drew in a deep breath, trying to calm the erratic beating of her heart. She looked deep into his eyes, searching the bronze-flecked brown as they became inky black.

'It's wrong because I promised Sebastian I would look after you.' He stepped back away from her, breaking the powerful spell and leaving her so weak she thought she might crumple on the floor. 'I did not promise to seduce his sister and right now that is all I can think of doing.'

Her breathing was becoming ever harder

to control, the sequin-encrusted bodice of the dress tightening with each attempt to breathe normally. He'd admitted he wanted her and her body hummed with a need she'd never known before, one that demanded satisfaction.

'We will be late.' She said the first thing that came to her mind to avoid confronting what sparked between them.

He laughed, a sound so sexy and throaty she blushed. Why had she said that?

'Is that an invitation, *cara*?' He pulled the cuff of his jacket back with long tanned fingers and looked at his watch. 'When I make love to a woman I take my time, give pleasure and enjoy it. You're right, if I take you back in there now we will be late. Very late.'

The smile on his lips, the invitation in his eyes were all too much, shocking her and giving her a much-needed reminder why she was even here with him. 'That can't happen, Alessandro. I'm not here to be your latest conquest.' Desperately, she tried to hide her desire, her confusion behind the words.

'Are you sure about that, *cara*?' He folded his arms across his broad chest and leant back against the wall, looking so handsome and sure of himself.

'You're impossible,' she fumed and turned towards the stairs, rushing down them so quickly her dress billowed out behind her and her heels tapped out an angry rhythm. His gentle laughter followed her, teasing and so sexy. She let out an exasperated groan.

Once at the bottom of the stairs, she pulled open the door of the building, drawing the warm early evening air deep into her lungs, wanting to banish the lustful throb that still hummed inside her. Seconds later, he was at her side, his hand in the small of her back, guiding her towards the door of the car as the driver opened it and stood back.

Swiftly, she got in, thankful of the roomy interior. At least she didn't have to sit close to him. But that roomy interior vanished as soon as he got in and, despite the expanse of leather seats between them, he felt too close. Her pulse, still unbalanced from that fleeting kiss, raced, making her light-headed.

She looked out of the window as the car pulled away, leaving the historic centre of Milan and the impressive Duomo behind. She feigned an interest in the passing streets she was far from feeling after their *encounter* outside his apartment. She couldn't trust herself to look at him, didn't want to see the hot desire in his eyes. Not now, on the night of the launch—a moment that was for her brother.

* * *

Relief surged through Alessandro as they reached the exclusive hotel where the launch party was being held. At least with other people around him he could distract himself. From the second he'd seen her, the red silk of her dress clinging to her narrow waist, enhanced further by all the red sequins, he'd been lost. Her one bare shoulder distracted him so completely that all thoughts of keeping her at a distance after the test track kiss had vanished.

He wanted her. More than he'd ever wanted any woman.

The driver opened his door and he got out amidst flashes from the waiting press and made his way around to Charlie's door. He held her hand as she stepped out, fighting the sizzle that shot through him from that contact. He didn't miss her hesitation as the photographers went crazy, flashes lighting up the ever darkening sky, their calls resounding around them.

'I hadn't expected so many,' he said sternly as she came to stand at his side. He should have warned her. Escaping the intrusion of the press had been her reason for retreating from the racing world and now she was in the thick of it again. 'Sorry, I didn't think to tell you they'd be here.'

'I expected it.' She smiled up at him, then faced the cameras as photographers shouted at them. 'Just not so many.'

He put his arm around her, pulling her close, feeling only a slight resistance as she continued to pose for the media. Seb had told him she was the best, knew just how to work the press to the team's advantage and, despite his doubts, he saw immediately this was true. But she was smiling and posing under duress and a tinge of guilt slipped over him.

The tension in her body increased and he turned her away from the press, heading into the hotel. All around, people chatted, sipping the champagne being circulated, but as they entered a hush fell on the room. Beside him, Charlie drew in a deep breath, straightened and as he looked across at her he saw a smile light up her face.

'I had not anticipated such a turnout.' He spoke softly, for her ears only. 'It seems you have many people wishing to meet you.'

'My presence here is a way of absolving you of any wrongdoing…in the eyes of the media and public, that is.' She whispered the words with her smile still in place and he suddenly saw how she must be feeling, how this whole evening must be for her.

'That was not my intention.' He placed his hand against her back, felt the heat and tried to ignore it.

'No, I don't think it was.' She looked up at him and, despite the smile on her lips, he knew that inside she was hurting. He could see it in her eyes and wanted to protect her from it.

She turned her attention to those around them, her smile easing the tension in the room, and a hum of conversation gradually started again. He took two flutes of champagne, handed her one and moved into the room, aware that every man there was looking at her with admiration.

A stab of jealousy spiked him, but instantly he dismissed it. She wasn't his and never could be. His urge to protect her and keep her at his side was thwarted as they were engaged in conversation before being separated.

Even though she was on the other side of the room, deep in conversation with several Italian racing drivers, he was aware of her. Each time she laughed, the gentle sound rippled through the air and he had to defuse the heady pulse of passion or he'd be in danger of dragging her away and doing just what his body demanded.

He made his welcome speech, repeating it in English for her benefit, but he couldn't look at her because if he did he wouldn't be able to stay here in front of everyone and remain calm. His prepared lines became jumbled and he improvised. Something he'd never had to do before.

'Now, to the moment everyone is waiting for,' he said as the doors of the hotel courtyard were folded back to reveal the shape of his car beneath a black cloth. Appreciative sounds came from those around him but, instead of giving the signal to pull off the cloth, he turned back to the audience.

Charlie looked up at him as he stood on the presentation stage, questions in her eyes, but he continued with his original plan.

'I'd like to introduce, for those who don't know her, Charlotte Warrington, sister of the late and very much missed Sebastian Warrington, who played a big part in developing this car.'

He turned, ignoring the need to look at her again, and gave the signal to reveal the car. Delighted sounds and applause came from everyone as the brilliant red of the car sparkled beneath the lights.

Finally he looked towards Charlie. She was slowly making her way towards the car, the red of her dress a perfect match for its gleaming paintwork, but the expression on her face sent alarm bells ringing. The smile she'd hidden behind from the moment she'd arrived in front of the cameras was gone. In its place was an expression of sadness that stilled the applause.

He stepped down and briskly made his way over to her, the audience parting ahead of him. He didn't know what to say, didn't know how to offer her support, and he cursed the fact that she'd only seen the plain grey test car until now.

'Charlotte?'

Slowly she turned to look at him. 'It's beautiful, Sandro.' The fact that she'd shortened his name didn't go unnoticed. All her barriers were down; she was exposed, vulnerable, and it was because of his carelessness.

'You were meant to see it yesterday afternoon.' She looked up at him, her eyes greener than he'd ever seen them. He didn't need to add that their test track kiss had thrown all his plans into disarray. Her expression and hint of a blush told him she knew why.

'Seb would be proud.' Her soft voice was firm and she turned to those around her, the smile she'd been using all night firmly back in place. The shutters had rolled back.

Charlie looked at Alessandro, blinking back the tears that momentarily threatened. 'Thank you.' Her voice was almost a whisper and, despite the throng of people around them, eager to get a good look at the car, it seemed as if it was only them there.

He moved closer, his eyes holding hers, and her heartbeat sped to an alarming rate. His height and broad shoulders made her feel small and defenceless but the intensity in his eyes cancelled that and she basked in his bold desire for her.

'Seb would also be proud of you.' His gentle words focused her attention back on the task at hand, giving her a chance to quell the almost primal need racing through her, need that only he could satisfy. 'You outshine the car.'

She laughed gently. 'That's not what I intended.' She hadn't. If she'd known the car was red she would have chosen a different colour dress, but red had been Seb's favourite. 'I should have known Seb would have wanted the car to be red.'

He didn't say anything and worry flitted through her. His mouth was set in a firm line and she used the offer of more champagne to dilute the tension between them. He followed her lead and took a flute, clinking it against hers as he raised it to her. 'To Seb.'

The tribute, spoken sternly, poured cooling water over the fire which was still raging inside her since the kiss a few hours ago outside his apartment. How did he manage to awaken her so completely yet still leave her yearning for more?

'To Seb.' She took a sip, her gaze remaining locked with his. Those flecks of bronze became more diluted as his eyes darkened again. Whatever was between them wasn't going away; it was intensifying. Each glance, each touch and definitely each kiss increased the sizzle of attraction.

She couldn't deny it any longer.

She didn't want to deny it.

She wanted to be with him, wanted to feel his lips on hers and keep kissing him. She craved his touch and caresses, needed to feel his body against hers. But men like Alessandro Roselli, who had looks and wealth on their side, never wanted more than a brief affair. She'd learnt that the hard way, rebounding from a broken relationship with her childhood boyfriend into the arms of an up-and-coming

racing driver, only to find he was using her to
further his career.

Despite that, she still wanted to explore
what was between them, but only if he didn't
want any kind of commitment from her. She
didn't want her heart exposed to pain. But
would one night be enough to quench the
thirst of desire?

'It's been a successful evening, *grazie*.' His
words dragged her attention back, his gaze a
soft caress and his words so tender and warm,
making her yearn to hear it as he kissed her
again and again.

'It's not over yet.' She couldn't believe she'd
said the words aloud, offering something she'd
only just realised she wanted. Judging by the
look of surprise on his face, neither could he.
But it was what she wanted, she realised as
she watched his expression change, riveted
to the spot by her bluntness. She wanted to
forget all reason and abandon herself to the
pleasure of his kisses, his caresses.

He raised his glass fractionally, not breaking eye contact, and her stomach twisted into
knots of excitement and apprehension. 'Then
I will drink to its continued success.' His rich
voice was vibrant and warmth surged through
her faster than lightning.

Shyness took over, banishing the boldness that had made her promise something she wanted but knew she shouldn't. She lowered her gaze and looked into her champagne as if the bubbles could give her the answers. 'Sorry, I shouldn't...'

Her words of apology, withdrawing her bold statement, were cut off by a familiar voice and she whirled around to see her father. He shook Alessandro's hand warmly and she marvelled at the ease with which they greeted one another.

'My flight was late.' Her father smiled at her, seemingly unaware of the tension between her and Alessandro. 'But I see you have done yourself—and Seb—proud.'

'I didn't know you were coming.' She sent up a silent prayer of thanks. Her father's arrival had stopped her from throwing herself at Alessandro and making a fool of herself into the bargain.

'I'm not staying. I will be leaving for Rome in a few hours, but I had to come and see you emerge like a butterfly back into the real world, and what a very beautiful butterfly you are.' He looked at her, his smile gentle, and she knew he really was proud and very pleased she'd stepped back into the limelight.

'So, the car—has it gone down well?' Her father turned to Alessandro and within minutes they were immersed in conversation. One she would normally relish hearing, but she needed to put space between her and Alessandro, cool things down. Maybe now it was time to mingle with potential buyers, do what she'd come here for.

Alessandro watched as Charlie talked animatedly with other people about the car, about its performance, and he recalled how well she'd driven it. She was more than qualified to sing its praises but it wasn't the drive, however fast, he was remembering. It was the kiss. Holding her in his arms and feeling her body against his.

Just a few guests lingered now, along with the racing drivers she'd been talking to earlier. Had she given them the same hints she'd given him? The way they hung on her every word certainly suggested as much.

An unknown need to be territorial made him stand as close to her as possible, but just doing so infused him once more with sizzling need. 'Thank you, gentlemen,' he said firmly, ignoring the way she shot him a startled glance. 'Any more questions you may have can be directed to my office.'

The remaining guests left, animated discussion of speed and performance trailing in their wake, but Alessandro watched Charlie as she leant back against the wing of the car, her red dress so perfect a match she almost became one with the slumbering beast.

Heat scorched through him as he remembered her earlier words and he undid his tie, letting it hang down, and pulled loose his top buttons. He'd never been so suffocated by desire before, had never experienced this continuous aching need.

He wanted her with a ferocious need, his promise to Seb becoming lost in the mists of heady desire. He should turn and walk away. To have kissed her at the test track had been so wrong. It had unlocked a thirst that needed quenching. Did she feel the same?

He looked at her and her eyes met his, darkening by the second. She smiled, a shy seductive smile that made his pulse leap. Instantly, he closed the distance between them, taking her in his arms and claiming her lips. She tasted better than ever; the anticipation of the last few hours had been worth the wait.

He caressed her cheek as he deepened the kiss, her response setting fire to his senses so instantly there was only one way to put out the flames now. Her skin was so soft and as his fingers caressed her bare throat he felt the wild pump of her pulse.

She wrapped her arms around his neck, her breasts pressing against his chest, and he moved her back against the car, pressing into her as heady lust robbed him of all thought.

'Sandro,' she murmured against his lips, pushing him almost too far.

It was all he could do to stop himself ripping the red dress from her, wanting to reveal her glorious body to his hungry gaze. Somewhere on the periphery sense prevailed.

This couldn't happen here and if he didn't stop kissing her there was a very real probability that it would. He pulled back from her, seeing her thick dark lashes flutter open to reveal eyes swirling with passion. 'My car is outside.'

Would she remember her covert promise to him that the night was still young? Her kiss certainly suggested as much, but did she want him enough to put all their differences aside for one night?

Shyly she looked up at him, a small sexy smile lifting her lips. Then, without further words, he took her hand and led her away from the car, through the brightly lit room where the hotel staff had started to clear up.

Movement caught his eye and he glanced over to see a photographer at a table, packing away his camera. Alessandro scrunched his eyes in suspicion, then, as her hand touched his arm, bringing her so close again, he dismissed the idea. He had far more important things to worry about than a rogue photographer.

He looked down into her upturned face as they stepped out into the warmth of the night, her smile reaching her eyes. 'It has been a very successful night,' she said as the car stopped outside the door.

'One I hope will continue in the same way.'

Demurely she looked down as he opened the car door. Once inside the car, he pulled her close against him, her head resting on his shoulder as if they'd known each other for ever. He didn't want to kiss her now. He didn't trust himself to be able to stop if things got heated. No, this was going to be played out in the comfort of his bedroom, where nothing and nobody could disturb them.

CHAPTER SEVEN

CHARLIE LIFTED THE front of her dress with one hand, the other still firmly in Alessandro's as they made their way up the marble staircase to his apartment. It was late and she should be tired. Last night she'd hardly slept and this evening she'd enjoyed the champagne just a little too much, but every sense in her body was on high alert.

Alessandro turned the key in the door and then looked at her, a seductive gentleness in his eyes. 'I want to kiss you again.' His voice was hardly above a whisper and his eyes searched her face.

He was so strikingly handsome, his tie hanging loosely and his white shirt open at the top button—exactly the romantic image that turned a girl's head. She smiled up at him, suddenly so sure that this was what she wanted. He wasn't the kind of man to want commitment and, for once in her life, neither did she. She wasn't looking or thinking beyond this moment.

'I shouldn't, but I do.' He moved closer, his height almost as overpowering as the tension that fizzed between them.

'Why shouldn't you?' Her voice was husky and she looked up at him, unsure what he meant.

'I promised Seb to look after you, not seduce you.' The resolute growl in his voice made her heart race faster than any car she'd driven.

'Seb wouldn't be cross.' She couldn't keep the light teasing note from her voice. He was fighting this attraction as much as she was, which made her want him even more. She wanted his kisses, his touch and to be totally his—tonight, at least

She wanted him more than she had wanted any other man and it scared her, but at least with Alessandro there wasn't any danger of anything more than a brief affair. The idea of getting involved in another relationship didn't appeal. She'd been hurt once before and that was enough. 'I want you to kiss me again, Sandro.'

'But if I do—' he lowered his voice and his eyes softened as he looked down at her '—I'm not going to be able to stop. Not this time.'

She walked away from him and into the apartment, feeling empowered by his desire for her. Slowly she turned as he shut the apartment door, its click ominous, warning her she'd passed the point of no return. But she didn't care. She didn't want to stop. Not now. This passion, which had ebbed and flowed between them since the moment they'd met, needed to reach its conclusion. There wasn't any other option now.

He might be the man she still saw as responsible for Seb's accident, even though her father didn't, but he was also the man who'd ignited a fire of hot need within her. From the second she'd seen him standing in her garden she'd fallen for him. This attraction was something she couldn't turn her back on. Not yet. It was a totally new experience for her.

'I don't want you to stop, Sandro.' The husky whisper that came from her sounded so unreal and she watched as he stepped towards her, his tie hanging loose, his shirt unbuttoned and the hint of golden skin of his chest creating an evocative image. One which seared into her mind and would, she knew, remain there for ever.

He took her hand once more and, with a seductive look which whispered a thousand words, he drew her towards him, pulling her close. '*Mia cara*, I have wanted you since the moment I first saw you.'

A tremor of panic slipped over her, his words too serious. Did he want more than just this moment, this night which held the promise of so much pleasure? It wasn't what she wanted. She couldn't give him more. She pushed her hands against his chest, the firmness of it making her breath catch, but she refused to let it sway her from what she had to say, what she had to make clear.

'I don't do for ever, Sandro.' She'd been sure all along he just wanted a fling, a brief affair. The image of her and Alessandro, together and happy in the future, didn't fill her mind. It was more than just risking her heart. It was about letting go of pain and grief and she wasn't ready to do that yet. But one night meant only putting it aside and not engaging her heart. 'It's all I can give you.'

'So serious, *cara*,' he said and pressed a light kiss to her forehead. 'Isn't my divorce proof that I'm not able to commit to a relationship? Tonight belongs to us, *cara*.'

Before he could say anything else she looked up, bringing his lips tantalisingly close to hers, the shock of discovering he was divorced dulled by the passion which sizzled inside her. It proved he didn't do forever either and all she wanted now was to lose herself in the moment, forget the world existed. 'Kiss me, Sandro.'

In answer he kissed her so gently she thought she might actually cry. His previous kisses had been hard and demanding, but this was so tender, so loving. He held her as if she were a delicate flower he was afraid he might crush. She swayed towards him, desire making her light-headed as he continued the kiss.

Just when she thought she couldn't stand the torment any longer he stopped kissing her and, with blatant intent, led her through to his bedroom. As with the rest of the apartment, old blended stylishly with new and the corner of the room comprised of windows offering unrivalled views of the Duomo, lit up and sparkling like a thousand jewels against the night sky. But all that was lost on her. All she could see was him.

'Un momento.' He released her hand and closed the cream curtains before flicking on the bedside lamps, creating a room for romance. Then he walked back towards her, slipping off his jacket as he did so and tossing it carelessly onto the armchair that filled another corner of the room.

'Wait,' she said and walked towards him, smiling coyly, her gaze meeting his from beneath her lowered lashes. With unashamed enticement she reached up, flattened her hands against his chest, revelling in the strength and his ragged intake of breath. Slowly she pulled one end of his tie until it fell from his neck. Holding it up, she dangled it in front of him like a trophy, her brows raised suggestively.

'Tease.' He reached out, took hold of her waist and pulled her against him, his hold keeping her there, leaving her in no doubt he wanted her.

Still believing she was in charge, she undid first one button of his shirt and, meeting no resistance, continued with each button until she was forced to gently pull the shirt from his trousers. As she unfastened the final buttons she slid her hands inside and over his chest. Hair covered his muscles, but couldn't hide them from her exploring hands. The heat of his body emboldened her further.

She looked at his face, his eyes so dark and heavy with desire that shivers of delight rushed over her. Very slowly she pushed open the shirt and kissed his chest, little kisses as light as a feather all over him, his musky scent invading her senses. She heard him groan with pleasure, his hold on her waist tightening, and she smiled.

She pulled back from him and pushed the

shirt from his shoulders. 'This has to go.' Her voice was husky and she almost didn't recognise it, but then she'd never done anything so bold before.

One-night stands had never been for her, not after the devastation caused to her parents' marriage, when her mother had succumbed to temptation. But this was different. Deep down, she acknowledged that if it had happened at a different time, in a different place it could have been so much more than one night.

She pushed that thought aside, refusing to allow it to defuse the sexual tension which filled the room.

He lifted his arms behind her as he unfastened the cuffs of his shirt, pressing her unbearably close. Before he released her, his lips pressed hard to hers, his breathing deep as his tongue slid into her mouth, teasing and tasting. She kissed him back, demanding more. For a moment his kiss matched hers, then abruptly he pulled back. 'The shirt?'

She smiled, feeling more brazen by the second. 'Yes, the shirt,' she whispered. 'It has to go.' She slid her hands up his chest, making him groan and close his eyes as she lingered there before pushing the white material from his shoulders. He moved first one arm from her, then the other and the shirt fell to the floor.

Again he pulled her close, but this time his fingers caught the zip at the back of her dress, slowly pulling it lower and lower; all the while his eyes held hers. Shyness swept over her and she resisted the urge to look away as his hand slid over her shoulder, pushing the one sleeve away and revealing her skin to his kisses.

The dress slipped down her body and slithered into a heap of silk and sequins at her feet. She stood against him, conscious of the fact that she now only wore the red underwear she'd bought to go with the dress and the strappy sandals she'd fallen in love with instantly.

Before she had time to think, he'd swept her off her feet and carried her to the bed. She lay where he'd placed her and looked up at him. He kicked off his shoes and was reaching for the fastener on his trousers when she knelt up on the bed and pushed his hands away. 'My turn.'

Who was this bold woman, this seductress? And why did it have to be this man who'd revealed her? This was a side of her she'd never known existed. Never before had passion taken over, making her want things with scant regard for the consequences.

A string of Italian that she was unable to understand flew from his lips as she opened his trousers, letting them slip down, leaving him in only a snug pair of black hipsters. As she looked up at him he caught her face between his hands and bent to kiss her. The spark was well and truly lit. Electricity shot between them. There would be no stopping now.

Before she had a chance to catch her breath he tumbled her onto the bed, his body pressing her into the softness of the covers. His kiss became urgent and demanding and she surrendered willingly to his domination.

His hands cupped her breast and inside her something exploded as she arched herself up to him, wanting his touch and so much more. Kisses trailed down her throat and she sighed in pleasure as her fingers slipped into the silky thickness of his hair. His tongue teased her nipple through the red lace of her strapless bra and her fingers tightened in his hair.

As if reading her urgent need, his hand slipped under her arched back, his fingers expertly flicking open her bra, releasing her breasts to his erotic kisses. Possessively he took a nipple in his mouth, swirling his tongue around it, making her cry out with pleasure. Moments later he moved his attention to the other nipple as his hand slid down her side and over her thigh, pulling her closer to the hardness of his erection.

'So beautiful,' he said huskily in between kisses and he moved back up her throat; the warmth of his body scorched hers until she felt as if flames licked around her.

She moved her hands down his back, savouring the latent strength beneath her fingertips. Lower she moved until she slipped her fingers in the back of his hipsters but, before she could make any attempt to remove them, he moved quickly onto his back, taking her with him until she sat astride him.

'That was…' she blushed beneath his open admiration, once again empowered by his need '…very masterful.'

His hands held her hips, keeping her exactly where he wanted her, and a hot stab of desire rushed over her. Following his need, she moved against him. With eyes as black as ebony he held her gaze until, drawn by something inexplicable, she lowered her body over him, bringing her lips against his.

'I am,' he said hotly between fast passionate kisses. 'Now, all night you will be mine.'

Charlie liked the sound of that; she wanted all night with him, wanted to enjoy this wonderful feeling again and again. 'Make me yours,' she whispered against his lips. 'Now.'

With the same suddenness of moments ago, she was once more lying on the bed, Sandro at her side. His fingers hooked into the lace of her panties and slowly pulled them lower, his eyes holding hers all the while.

She quivered as his fingers moved back to touch her, closed her eyes as a wave of pleasure rushed over her like the tide washing over the sand, taking her higher, almost to the point of no return. He took her lips in a hard and bruising kiss, his tongue as demanding as his touch, and her breath came hard and fast. It was too much and not enough both at the same time, leaving her wanting more.

Just when she'd almost slipped over the edge he pulled away from her. She opened her eyes, looking up at him and blinking against the pounding and unsatisfied passion of her body. He reached across her and roughly pulled open the drawer of the cabinet beside the bed.

Of course. Protection. How had she not thought of that? His eyes met hers, a knowing light in their depths, as if he knew she'd almost lost control. She watched as he dispensed with his underwear and rolled on the condom. Anticipation zinged through her and a pulse of heady need throbbed heavily between her legs.

He moved over her and she opened to him, wanting him deep inside her, but he paused. Propped up on his hands, his muscles straining with the effort, he looked down at her, his breathing deep and fast.

'Sandro?' She couldn't keep the question from her voice. Was he having doubts? What had she done?

Then his mouth claimed hers in a hungry and possessive kiss as he pushed into her, taking himself in deeply. She gasped against his lips, his kiss smothering the sound as he moved inside her, sending firecrackers of explosion all around her.

She moved with him, taking him deeper still. He dropped down against her, his warm skin pressing against her body as he kissed her neck, his hands grasping her hair tightly. A flurry of hoarse Italian erupted from him as he thrust harder, sending her over the edge and beyond. Further than she'd ever been before.

She dug her nails into his back, moving with him as the ecstasy crashed into her. His grip on her hair tightened as he gasped out his release and kissed her hard. Then, as the heady lust ebbed slowly away, their bodies tangled, she wrapped her arms around him, keeping him against her, and softly kissed the dampness of his face.

She'd just experienced something she'd never before known and wanted to hold onto the moment just a little longer.

Alessandro could hardly think, the beat of his pulse was so loud. He couldn't move; every muscle in his body had been weakened by the power of hers. She kissed his face and he closed his eyes against the tenderness of that kiss. It was too intimate, too loving and he didn't deserve it.

He didn't deserve any of this and had almost stopped, but his name on her lips, husky and seductive, had made that impossible. Quickly he pushed aside the guilt. She'd wanted this as much as he had, leading the seduction like a temptress.

In a bid to hide the turbulent emotions racing through him, he propped himself up over her and looked down into her flushed face. 'You make love as wildly as you drive.'

She trailed her fingertips over his chest and looked up at him, coyness and temptation filling those emerald-green eyes. 'Are you going to insist I stop again?'

He should do—this wasn't what he'd imagined when he'd promised Seb he'd look out for his little sister, but then he hadn't expected to be so attracted to her and certainly he'd never have guessed at the passion hidden within her.

Gently he kissed her, tenderness that he hadn't felt for such a long time filling him. She responded, her kiss telling him that the fire of passion still burned within her, as it did inside him. He needed to cool things down, needed to calm the riot of emotions which raged within him. Emotions that were so intense and completely unwelcome.

'*Sì*. For now.' He pushed his protesting body away from hers, trying to ignore the wounded look on her beautiful face. Before he had a chance to question his motives, he left the bed and made his way to the bathroom.

Moments later, his face stinging from the cold water he'd splashed over it, he returned to the bedroom, but the bed was empty, the rumpled covers the only hint of the passion that had just played out there.

A rustle caught his attention and he looked towards the door where, clutching the red silk dress against her nakedness, Charlie stood. She was running away again. Was this what she always did? He should let her walk away—every rational sense inside him shouted the advice—but the hot-blooded man she'd resurrected wasn't about to let her slip away from him now.

He strode over to her, heedless of his nakedness and empowered by the shock and need that filled her eyes. She still desired him, just as he desired her. This passion wasn't spent yet.

'Come back to bed, Charlotte.' His voice was deep and raw, leaving him with the distinct impression that his emotions were as naked as he was.

'But...'

He silenced the hoarse whisper by tilting her chin up and kissing her lips, still swollen from his earlier kisses. She sighed and kissed him, dropping the dress carelessly to the floor. He pulled back but still held her chin and looked deep into her eyes, saw the green darken to resemble the heart of the forest, hidden from the sun.

'Tornare a letto, cara.' He brushed his lips on hers as a frown of confusion slipped over her face. Desire rushed through him and all he could think about was making love to her again and again. This might not be for ever, but it was certainly for now and, as far as he was concerned, *now* would last all night. 'Come back to bed, *cara.*'

* * *

Charlie all but melted at his feet, almost as crumpled as the sea of red silk on the floor between them. The raw and potent desire in his eyes couldn't be ignored. Neither could the kiss that promised so much more. She couldn't deny she wanted him. She knew she shouldn't and briefly wondered if this was how it had been for her mother. Had her mother been drawn inexorably towards the flame of desire, a flame that had then extinguished all the love she'd had for her husband, Charlie's father?

'Don't look so worried, *cara*.' His soft words broke her thoughts. Now was not the time to worry about the past. Unlike her mother, she wasn't married or committed in any way. She was free to enjoy this for what it was, a short and passionate affair.

But what of Seb? What would he have said? Hurriedly, she pushed that thought to the back of her mind, remembering what she and Sandro had enjoyed earlier. Seb had always wanted her to be happy and right now her whole body was alive with happiness.

She smiled at Sandro as he took her hand and led her back to the bed, the passion that had raged between them earlier beginning to heat again. Desperate to drown her misgivings, she wrapped her arms about his neck, pressing herself against his nakedness, and kissed him as if her life depended on it.

Suddenly he tumbled her back on the bed, his body over hers as his hot kisses stoked the fire of passion ever higher and she was lost once more.

CHAPTER EIGHT

'*BUONGIORNO.*' THE SOFT Italian greeting stirred her senses and Charlie opened her eyes. Sunlight poured in around the closed curtains, but all she could focus on was the man beside her. Every limb in her body was replete with Alessandro's lovemaking and she stretched, smiling up at him, enjoying the way his eyes clouded with passion. 'Breakfast awaits.'

'Breakfast? How long have I slept?' She sat up, pulling the soft sheet modestly against her. He stood by the bed, dressed in jeans which hugged his strong thighs and a black T-shirt which highlighted the contours of his chest to perfection.

His gentle laugh knotted her insides and she dragged her gaze from him, to look at the clock which ticked beside the bed. 'Long enough, *cara*, but then we didn't sleep much last night.'

She turned quickly to look at him, heat infusing her cheeks as his words confirmed her memory was correct. Was it all over now— the one night of passion she'd willingly entered into? Was this now time to go back to her room, to return to the professional relationship they'd had initially? There was still more promotion scheduled for the car over the weekend and into the following week. How was she going to get through the weekend after what they'd shared last night?

'Thank you.' She was confused by the way she felt and the need to distance herself from him. Wanting to return to the businesslike dealings they'd had with one another until last night. 'I'll get dressed, then we can discuss what's next on the promotion agenda.'

'Oh, no, *cara*. There is only one thing on the agenda right now.' A teasing smile lingered on his lips and the suggestive tone of his voice made her stomach flutter wildly. He still wanted her.

Her heart thumped as he strode back to stand beside the bed. Her mouth was as dry as a desert and she tried to moisten her lips but, from the smouldering look in his eyes, that was a mistake. 'There is?' The strangled whisper only just managed to squeeze out.

He leant on the bed, so close that her lips parted without her consent, waiting for his kiss. When it came it was soft and teasing and loaded with promise. She closed her eyes, slipping under his masterful spell far too easily. 'I'm taking you somewhere we can be alone, somewhere we can explore what is between us.'

She pulled sharply back from him. 'But the launch…the promotion? You're supposed to be hosting a promotional afternoon at the test track.' She'd already expressed a wish to be there and was torn between the idea of spending time alone with him and being with the car her brother had designed.

'Someone else can handle that.' He moved towards her again, stretching his body across the bed, making her want to reach out and touch him, feel his strength. 'We have far more important things to do.'

'But…' She raised her hand, pressing it against his shoulder, stopping him coming any closer. The sheet she'd pulled against her slipped down, exposing her breasts, but she held her ground, keeping a firm expression on her face.

His eyes looked down at her, his appreciative gaze sending heat to the centre of her again, and her breath hitched audibly as if he'd caressed her. '*Per Dio*, but you are so hard to resist.' His accent became heavy and she released his shoulder and clutched the sheet quickly against her once more, shyness rushing over her now that daylight flooded the room.

'It was only meant to be one night, Sandro.' Her voice was barely above a whisper and she felt emotionally exposed and vulnerable.

'You need to stop running, Charlie, and face what scares you.' His body, tall and overpowering, dominated the room but his expression was gentle. Did he understand her fears? Empathise with her?

She looked up at him, willing the carefree attitude she'd had last night to infuse her again. With alarming clarity she realised she was using not just Seb's accident but her disastrous love life as a shield. Retreating behind it and potentially denying herself more pleasure than she could imagine.

'I want to be at the test track.' She injected a firmness she was far from feeling into her voice and, from the look on his face, he knew she was already running.

'It is not necessary, not after last night.' He stood back up, his height dominating the room. 'We will spend the weekend at my villa. I intend to explore what you started last night, enjoy it. Do you not feel the same, *cara*?'

Should she lie? Tell him she didn't want to

be with him any more when the heat of her body and the pounding of her heartbeat told her she did? She slipped from the bed, dragging the sheet she clutched with her. 'What about the car?'

'The car will still be there on Monday.' His voice was deep and the darkness of his eyes told her he wasn't thinking about the car at all.

He was right. The car would still be there after the weekend, but the passion which still burned fiercely between them wouldn't be. She didn't want it to be anything more than a brief affair. This way, it would burn itself out, enabling her to concentrate on what she'd come to Italy for. The truth about Seb's accident.

'Just the weekend.' She smiled at him, enjoying the power she seemed to have over him. 'But no more.'

'Bene.' He moved to the door of the bedroom, filling it with his oh-so-sexy body, and she could hardly think. 'We leave in an hour.'

Alessandro revved the car along the open road, the bustle of Milan far behind them, but tension still filled him. He'd seen the panic in her eyes as she'd sat in the bed, but he'd also seen the desire. Whatever was holding her back hadn't been quite strong enough and he sensed it was more than just her brother. That was only a smokescreen.

His body longed for the moment he could make her his again, but he questioned if he was right to do so. If he was a betting man he'd stake everything on the fact that Seb had never intended this to happen when he'd made Alessandro promise what now turned out to be impossible. How could he possibly look after Charlie when all he wanted to do was make love to her again and again?

Inwardly he cursed. The idea behind bringing her to his villa was to be somewhere the ghost of her brother's memory couldn't reach. Whatever had happened last night wasn't about Seb—or the car. It was about them and the hot lust which zipped between them from just one look. After last night the temperature of that lust had risen instead of cooling, as he'd thought it would have done.

'*Benvenuti* Villa Dell Angelo.' Pushing his doubts and thoughts of Seb aside, he pulled off the road and into the driveway of his villa, perched on the hillside. Beyond it, Lake Garda glittered like a thousand jewels in the midday sun. This was his new place of sanctuary and Charlie was the first woman he'd ever brought here.

'It's beautiful.' Her soft gasp of pleasure

did untold things to his body and he tried to keep his mind on the here and now instead of roaming back to last night or fast forwarding to the pleasures that would await him as darkness fell once more.

'Sì, grazie.' He stopped the car, turned off the engine and looked across at her. 'But not as beautiful as you.'

She blushed and dropped her gaze, amazing him that a woman who had been so bold in the bedroom just hours ago could be so shy from his compliment. That boldness did, however, salve his conscience and ease the guilt he felt at breaking his promise. Whilst it was true he had needed little invitation last night, she had instigated it, even warning him she didn't do for ever. She'd wanted last night as much as he had, despite the innocent blushes which now coloured her cheeks.

He got out of the car before he gave in to the temptation to kiss her again. 'I have arranged for lunch on the terrace, then we will drive down to the local town of Desenzano for the afternoon, maybe take a ferry across the lake.' If he didn't take her out he knew they would spend the whole afternoon in bed and, whilst the sex was amazing, he wanted to know her better. That thought shocked him and he frowned as he watched her taking in the view. She was beginning to get to him, tear down his wall of protection.

'Sounds lovely.' Her heels tapped out a gentle beat as she walked towards the terrace, the warm wind pressing her white sundress against her body, making him draw in a sharp breath as he fought for control. He'd never been this affected by a woman before, not even the woman he'd married, foolishly believing he loved her.

'I'm glad you approve,' he said with a smile as he watched her walk and pushed the memories from the past to the back of his mind where they belonged.

Charlie couldn't help but stop as they rounded the corner of the ornate villa. A large infinity pool stretched away, blending with the views of the lake far below, becoming one with it. Under the shade of trees, a table was laid out for lunch, looking so luxurious she felt as if she'd stepped into another world. This was on another level to the glamour her career had showed her so far. It was pure indulgence.

'If we take a ferry maybe we should do a little exploring before returning to dine in Desenzano.' He gestured her to sit and then took his seat opposite her. Beyond him the view seduced her almost as much as the man himself and she tried hard to keep her mind focused on the here and now, instead of allowing it to drift towards thoughts of what their time together would bring.

'And then?' What was the matter with her? Why did she need to act the seductress still? *Because that's what you were last night and that's what he's expecting.* The reprimand shot swiftly through her mind. She had been brazen, but they'd both agreed this was just an affair, a short dalliance. Right now she might be someone she'd never been before, but that didn't mean she couldn't enjoy it. Once it was over and the launch complete she would return to her life in England and try to move on.

He raised his brows, leant back in his chair and smiled—a slow lazy smile that was so sexy she almost couldn't breathe—but his next words made that breath catch in her throat. 'Then we spend the night making love.'

His bluntness shocked her, but she smiled teasingly back at him, enjoying the freedom to be different from normal. It was as if he'd unlocked a new and completely unexpected version of herself, one that lived a carefree and happy existence. 'Promises, promises.'

'All night, *cara*, you will be mine, that I do promise, but first we eat.' He watched her with a steadfast gaze that dissolved the few remaining doubts which lingered in her mind. He wanted her, she wanted him. Was it so wrong to put aside everything else and enjoy the mutual attraction until it fizzled out?

It *was* wrong. It went against everything she believed in. She didn't do affairs and certainly didn't want a relationship with anyone and definitely not with Alessandro, but the connection between them was impossible to ignore. For the first time in her life she was throwing caution to the wind, almost seeing it being snatched away to float above the blue waters of the lake.

She picked up her glass of wine and lifted it to him. 'To tonight,' she toasted, enjoying the smile that tugged at his lips and the hum of anticipation that warmed her body.

'Salute!' He raised his glass to her and she watched his eyes become as black as midnight, the desire-laden and smouldering look on his face making her heart constrict and her body heat.

The ferry from Desenzano to Sirmione offered a cool breeze which was a welcome relief from the heat of the afternoon. Charlie, feeling like a child, wanted to sit at the front of the paddle steamer to gain a prime view of the lake and surrounding countryside and

Alessandro seemed happy to indulge her. He made her feel special and cherished with his attention.

Passengers chatted and laughed all around them but still she felt as if she were in a bubble, just the two of them, wrapped up in the attraction which sizzled stronger than ever between them. He put his arm around her as they sat, pulling her close, and the moment took on a magical quality, as if they were in love and not just lovers.

In love.

The words rang in her mind. It couldn't be possible to be in love so soon. She was just being seduced by the sunshine, the luxury of this life she'd stepped into, but most of all by the man himself. Love didn't just happen. It grew and flourished within a happy relationship and this wasn't a relationship. It was an affair.

'I suppose this is a regular trip for you.' She tried to quell the unease of her emotions and distract her thoughts. She was probably just one of many. A man like Alessandro would never be short of female company.

'I bought the villa a year ago but have been too busy with the car to use it.' He looked ahead of them, the wind playing in his hair, his eyes hidden by dark glasses, then suddenly he turned to look at her. She saw herself reflected in his sunglasses and hated that she couldn't see the expression in his eyes.

'Did Seb ever come here?' The light question made his mouth set in a firm line and she wondered what she'd said wrong.

'No. It's why I brought you here. I wanted it to be just the two of us. No memories. There will be enough of those when we return to Milan.' His voice was hard and the clipped edge to it warned her off further questions.

He had at least confirmed one thing. This was still nothing more than a weekend affair. Once they were back in Milan it would be over and just a few days after she would leave for England and the life she needed to get back together. A brief affair was all she'd wanted, so why did it hurt to know she could so easily be dispensed with?

'I'm glad you brought me here. It has been a hard year and right now I feel I have a reprieve from thinking about Seb and the accident,' she said honestly. Certain aspects of her time in Italy had been painful. 'It's time to put the past behind me.'

The sound of the ferry's motor as it manoeuvred towards the shore halted further conversation, something she was grateful for. She didn't want to admit to him he'd been right, that being at the launch was not just what Seb had wanted but what she'd wanted.

She looked ahead of her as the ferry docked with a bump. The medieval castle dominating the town of Sirmione as it rose up from the blue waters of the lake unleashed a childlike need to explore. She pushed aside all other thoughts, determined to enjoy the day and Alessandro's company. 'I can't believe you've never been here or done this,' she said as she stood up, trying to lighten the mood.

'No, but now I will share the experience with you.' The smile on his lips almost melted her heart; it was far hotter than the sun. As the holiday-makers scurried off the ferry he pulled her into his arms and kissed her. The passion in that kiss must have been obvious to anyone who saw them, but she didn't care. All she wanted was to lose herself in his desire, to enjoy the short time they would have together before reality intervened.

'Sandro,' she murmured against his lips as her eyes fluttered open.

'We need to go now.' His voice was gravelly. He lifted his sunglasses onto his head and looked into her eyes, leaving her in no doubt as to why they had to go.

He took her hand and led her off the ferry. A knowing smile from a crew member was cast their way, making her blush again. Could everyone tell how much they wanted one another?

'The castle is the place to see,' he said as they walked alongside the walled moat of the impressive building. Swans moved gracefully over the rippling water and she wished she could be as free as them. Free to let go and love, to pair for life. But she couldn't, and certainly not with Sandro. She'd set the boundaries and he'd set the time limit. They would be lovers—for the weekend only.

Swept along with the tourists, they walked over the long bridge towards the impressive arched entrance and into the courtyard of the castle, its thick and high walls offering respite from the sun. He pulled her close, his arm around her waist, and she shivered, but not from being in the shade.

She feigned an interest in the history which oozed from the walls, desperate not to look at him or show just how much she wanted him. With his arm around her, they walked slowly over the cobbled courtyard and towards the steps up to the wall. As they reached the top, applause and cheers caught her attention and she turned to look back down into the courtyard, where a radiant bride posed with her new husband for photographs.

'Wouldn't it be fantastic to be married here?' She said the words aloud, without thinking how they would sound to him.

'If you find the right partner, yes.' His brittle words snagged her attention but she didn't look at him; instead she kept her attention on the happy scene playing out below them—a scene she'd always secretly hankered after. That was until her mother had destroyed all faith in fairy tales and happy ever afters.

'Sorry.' She was. A moment ago they'd been happy—smiling, laughing and kissing like lovers without a care in the world—and now she'd said the wrong thing.

'You have nothing to be sorry about, *cara*. Mine was a marriage that should never have happened. We were too young and wanted such different things.' She glanced at him to see that he too was watching the happy couple, his face set in hard lines of repressed anger.

'Love can deceive all of us,' she said and leant against the railings, preferring to look at him instead of the bride and groom.

'It wasn't love.' He snapped the words out and looked down at her. 'It was deception.'

'Deception?'

'We had known each other since childhood,' he began, keeping his attention focused on the events unfolding in the castle courtyard. 'It stood the test of time when I moved to Milan. Marriage seemed the normal progression and very much expected by our families.'

'So what went wrong?' She asked the question quietly, sensing his simmering anger.

'It wasn't me she really wanted, but the lifestyle she thought I could give her. What she hadn't accounted for in her scheming was that I would be putting every last cent back into my uncle's business. She soon tired of my frugal ways and found a man who could give her what she wanted.'

Charlie touched his arm, compelled to reach out, and he turned quickly to look at her, his eyes hard and glacial. She understood his feelings of betrayal. They almost mirrored hers.

For a moment he was silent, looking at her with unguarded curiosity. She held his gaze, trapped by the intensity of it.

'Seb told me you were once engaged.' Her heart plummeted but she smiled up at him, keeping her expression emotionless.

'Yes and, like you, we were too young. I was also far too naïve.' The sudden need to talk about something she'd hidden away surprised her. Was it his honesty that had triggered it? Whatever was happening between them, she was conscious of the earlier buoyant mood deflating as vulnerabilities were exposed. 'Let's not talk about it now; let's just enjoy our time together.'

'That is why you don't do for ever? Your heart has been broken?' He ignored her attempt to change the subject and lifted her chin with his fingers, brushing a kiss on her lips, sending her already distracted body into overdrive.

'I'd much prefer a wildly passionate affair,' she lied and moved closer to him, pressing her lips against his. A broken heart was only part of it and for the first time she realised what was really holding her back. What if she had the same capability to leave as her mother had?

'My sentiments exactly.' He deepened the kiss and she was vaguely aware of people passing them on the walkway and the wedding celebrations below moving away.

'Come on, let's explore.' Finally she pulled away from him, a teasing note in her voice. A little bit of distance between them was needed. Her heart was pounding and imagining all sorts of happy-ever-after scenarios with him.

'We shall go back a much faster way,' he said as they emerged from the castle, his voice full of laughter but the intent in his words clear. 'I've arranged for a private trip back; that way I can kiss you without feeling the world is watching.'

Excitement fizzed inside her at the thought of being alone with him but, as they stepped into the small speedboat waiting within the moat of the castle, the reality was very different. It was compact, forcing them close together, but it also meant they were very near to the driver.

Heat from Sandro seeped into her as she sat next to him. The boat made its way under the small castle bridges which reminded her of Venice, out of the medieval port and onto the lake. Soon they were speeding across the water and quickly she knotted her hair into a ponytail as they rushed back towards the small town of Desenzano. Alessandro pulled her tight against him and she closed her eyes, relishing the rush of air past her as the boat sped along and the feel of his strength. This was like a dream, so romantic and loving it would be easy to get carried away.

'I have a table booked at the best lakeside restaurant,' Alessandro said as the power-boat slowed and pulled alongside the quay. Flags flapped erratically in the wind and she grabbed her hair again with one hand to stop it from blowing all over her face as he took the other and helped her from the boat.

Time was passing too quickly. It hardly seemed possible they'd been together all day, but already the sun was slipping lower in the sky. Once dinner was over they would go back to his villa, a thought which sent shivers of anticipation zipping rapidly through her.

All through dinner Alessandro had fought the urge to take her back to his villa. The tension had mounted rapidly, almost to boiling point. She felt it too, of that he was sure, and, as she'd sipped her coffee, her eyes became as dark as moss, suggestion in their depths as to what the night would bring.

They were kindred spirits, both healing from failed relationships, both wanting only the here and now. But, as they made their way back to his car, he imagined what it would be like to be with Charlie every day, to spend weekend after weekend like this.

Such thoughts had to be stamped out. She didn't do for ever, she'd made that perfectly clear, and the promise he'd made Seb to look after her as if she were his sister loomed over him, mocking him as his desire for the one woman he couldn't have raged ever stronger.

Now he powered the car along the road, the

setting sun casting an orange glow all around them. He'd enjoyed his day with her but he knew he would enjoy the night much more. Here in his villa he was free to let go and love her. No promises hung over him, taunting him with guilt at what he was doing. Hurt from the past couldn't reach him any more and for just one more night she was his.

He sensed her watching him and glanced over at her. Did she guess at his eagerness to get her home?

'We have all night, Sandro.' She smiled lightly but the passion in her eyes told a very different story, as did the sexy purr when she said his name.

Would it be enough? he asked himself as he turned into the driveway of the villa, the last glimmer of the sun slipping beneath the horizon before them. Sunrise would mean their last day. They could only be lovers for the weekend. A weekend that was drawing rapidly to a close.

'*Ma per amare una donna...*' He tried hard to bring English to the fore as images of them together made his pulse race. Finally he managed to. 'But to love a woman like you I need more than one night.'

She reached up and touched his face, her fingertips snagging over his light growth of stubble. 'We only have tonight, Sandro. This can never be anything more. We don't belong together.'

Reminded of her earlier warning, he caught her hand and kissed her palm. 'Tonight only, but it will be one you will remember for ever.'

CHAPTER NINE

IF THAT FIRST morning waking in Alessandro's bed had been amazing, this morning was delicious. Charlie luxuriated against the warmth of his body like a kitten, content and sleepy. She lingered on the edge of sleep a moment longer, her back against his chest and his arms possessively keeping her close.

It was bliss and she didn't want to wake and face the day. Their last day together, and after their night of hot passionate sex she wasn't sure she wanted to begin the day. Birdsong drifted in through the open balcony doors and finally she opened her eyes to see the soft linen curtains stirring gently in the breeze.

It was like a dream, her body still singing from the hours of lovemaking, and now she felt safe. Loved. It was something she could get used to, but she mustn't. Thoughts of love drifted perilously close to the surface and she pushed them aside, aware something had changed. Deep down she wanted to be loved, but her disastrous engagement made that almost impossible. *This is just a weekend affair*, she reminded herself sternly as his arms pulled her tighter against him.

'Would you care to join me for a morning swim?' His lips brushed against the back of her neck and a flutter of butterflies took flight in her stomach. She closed her eyes against the heady sensation, ignoring her doubts of moments ago. It was still the weekend and still time to enjoy this affair.

'I don't have anything to wear.' She wished she did. The pool had looked inviting in the morning sun yesterday, but the thought of Sandro in it too made it infinitely better.

'Not a problem.' He kissed her ear and whispered to her, 'We are totally alone; nobody can see us.'

She turned in his arms, her pulse rate leaping wildly at the thought of swimming naked with him. 'Are you sure? No staff.'

'No staff. Nobody except you and me.' His words were heavy with accent and much more, making her body sing with desire she thought had long since been quenched.

He pulled her against him but she pushed at his chest with her hands, delighting in the chance to tease him again. 'I thought you wanted to swim.'

'I've changed my mind.'

In one swift move she leapt from the bed, the shock on his face making her laugh. Suggestively, she raised her brows. 'Well, I'm going for a swim.' Not wanting to pass up on the opportunity of such a luxurious pool, she rushed through the open balcony doors and down the stone steps that led to the pool. She glanced around briefly, checking they were as alone as he'd said, acutely aware she was still totally naked.

Without waiting to see if he followed, she dived into the cool blue water, glided forward then broke the surface. The sense of freedom was immense and she struggled to comprehend how just a bikini could hinder the feel of water against the skin. Only a short time ago she had been asleep but now her whole body was alive, invigorated by the cool water and the prospect of Alessandro joining her.

It was already warm. She swam to the end of the pool and, with her arms over the edge, looked out over Lake Garda as it stretched out below her. The sun's morning rays cast a golden glow over the tree-covered hills and mountains and already she could see the ferries, like tiny white shapes on the water, as they started their daily cruises.

Behind her she heard a small splash and moments later felt the water ripple against her neck as Alessandro dived in. She smiled but continued to survey the view, waiting with anticipation for him to join her. Her body trembled and her heart rate soared as she heard his strong strokes through the water. Then he was beside her, his arms on the edge, looking at the view too.

Embarrassment filled her. Swimming naked was not something she had ever done before and yet here she was, naked in Alessandro's pool. With breathing becoming difficult and her heart thumping hard, she needed to divert her attention, cool things down. She didn't even dare look at him.

'Stunning, isn't it?' She really couldn't believe she was here, enjoying a weekend of total luxury with the sexiest man she'd ever met.

'Semplicemente bellissimo.' Whenever he spoke Italian she got shivers of excitement down her spine, but this time she was certain he wasn't referring to the view and she turned to face him.

Shyness rushed over her at her nakedness and the hungry look in his eyes. She tried to mask it with bravado. 'Race you.' Without waiting to see if he'd taken up her challenge, she pushed away from the side of the pool, propelling herself through the water before beginning to swim back towards the villa.

Just as moments ago, she sensed him coming closer. Splashes of water landed around her as his strong arms carried him past her and to the end of the pool. His hand on the edge, his bronzed shoulders glistening in the morning sun, he waited for her to draw closer.

'I should have known you'd win.' She breathed out the words after the exertion of a brisk swim. Of course he'd win. She doubted he ever lost—at anything.

'You shouldn't challenge me, *cara*.' His voice was mocking and, without thinking, she splashed water at him, laughing in a way she hadn't laughed for a long time. 'And you shouldn't splash me either.'

Before she could do anything more, he hauled himself out of the water and effortlessly sprang to his feet to stand on the side of the pool looking down at her. She couldn't help but look at him and as her eyes travelled downwards shock set it.

'You cheat!' The words rushed from her as she took in the trunks clinging to him, water dripping from them. 'You tricked me. You let me believe we would both be naked.'

She hung on to the side of the pool, embarrassment colouring her cheeks. The smile on his face was too much. 'I never mentioned that I would be naked. Now, are you coming out or not?'

'Not.' She pouted up at him then swam slowly away, knowing he would be looking at her body.

She looked over at him as she swam, saw him grab a towel from a lounger and ruffle his hair dry, then stretch out on the lounger, watching every move she made. Her pulse rate went into overdrive.

'Do you make a habit of this, Miss Warrington?' His teasing question irritated her, yet made her smile too. He was playing games with her, toying with her like a cat did a mouse.

'Swimming naked or passionate weekend affairs?' She tossed the question at him as she reached the end of the pool, this time turning her back on the view of Lake Garda. There was a much more interesting view to take in now.

'Both.'

'I've never swum naked before.' She pushed away from the side, this time on her back, revelling in the chance to tease him just a bit, making her feel that little bit more in control. She had never had an affair, no matter how long, but she wasn't going to tell him that. She was tiring as she reached the end of the pool again but didn't want to come out of the water, not whilst he watched her so intently.

'I've never had a naked woman in my pool before.' His look was playful and the smile that moved his lips incredibly sexy.

She looked over at him, liking the way the sun gleamed in his damp hair. His long legs were as tanned as the rest of him and she feasted on the image he created, adding it to the one from their first night together, storing it away. This would be a scene never to be repeated.

'Well, that does surprise me. A man like you.' She kept her voice light and flirty, trying to echo his mood, but her heart was racing as heady need spread through her.

'A man like me?' He leant forward on the lounger, placing one foot on the floor. 'Just what is a man like me?'

She wished the words unsaid but continued with her carefree tone as she slowly swam to the side of the pool, holding the edge in front of him and trying to hide her nakedness. 'Don't try to deny you don't have women dropping at your feet.'

'Only those who are looking for something I can't give.' The brusque words, in complete contrast to his sexy and carefree stance, made her smile.

'Oh, and what's that?' she said, laughing teasingly at him.

'Marriage and security.' The air stilled around them and his mouth hardened just enough to warn her she'd strayed into dangerous territory. He sat back in the lounger again, as if to get as far away from the conversation as possible. Yesterday he'd talked of the end of his marriage to his childhood sweetheart. Was that the reason he'd never settled down again? She could certainly relate to that.

'And you don't want that?' She rested her arms on the side of the pool and looked at him, seeing an array of emotions flash across his face.

'No.'

The word was so final a chill slipped over her despite the warm sun on her back. She moved in the water, rippling sounds filling the heavy silence, but she couldn't look away, couldn't break the eye contact.

'I totally understand.' She did, but wished

she'd kept that to herself as his eyes narrowed suspiciously.

'You do?'

'Oh, you know, once bitten, twice shy, as we say in England.' She turned her back and swam away from him, not wanting this discussion she had inadvertently started. They should be enjoying their last hours together, not mulling over the past.

'You shouldn't hide from it, Charlie.' She stopped swimming as he said the very same words her father often said. Treading water, she turned to face him and swam back to the side of the pool, wishing she was wearing something so she could get out—of the pool and the conversation.

'Hide from what, Sandro?'

'Love.'

She blinked in shock, not quite able to believe a man who freely admitted to not wanting commitment would even use that word. 'I'm not hiding from it. I just haven't found it yet.'

'And when you do?'

She couldn't understand where the questions were coming from. She'd made it clear she didn't do for ever, so why channel the conversation this way? 'My mother left us as teenagers, Sandro. She left my father, turning her back on us. I haven't believed in happy ever after since.'

'And the man you were engaged to? Did you love him and dream of living happily ever after?' His scrutiny was intense and she hated the feeling of being trapped in the pool, forced to answer his questions.

'Maybe I wasn't ready to love after that.' That statement stunned her and she blinked against the admission, realising the truth of it.

'And if you were to fall in love?' His dark eyes fixed hers and she clutched harder to the side of the pool.

'If I was sure I'd found a man to love, one who would love me, then I might just think about for ever.'

'So you'd get married?' His voice rose in question and disbelief.

'Marriage isn't the only way to have love, Sandro.' He furrowed his brows speculatively at her and she turned the heat on him, deflecting it from herself. 'What about you—would you marry again?'

Alessandro looked down at Charlie, her wet hair slicked back from her face, highlighting the beauty of her eyes. She was stunning, but she was also talking of things he'd begun to question as he'd held her sleeping body against him this morning.

He'd been adamant he was done with love, done with marriage, but such thoughts had begun to filter from the back of his mind. Images of him and Charlie, sharing love and happiness, lingered on the edge, hazy images that hadn't yet become sharp and focused. Images that shouldn't even be there.

Just as he had done as she'd curled against him and slept, he wondered what it would be like to wake every morning, take her in his arms and kiss her awake. In just a few days she'd weaved a spell so potent he didn't want to let her go. Because she still blamed him for Seb's accident, he couldn't ask for more—not until he cleared himself of blame in her eyes. And he couldn't do that without telling her everything. And that would break his promise to Seb.

'Your silence says it all.' Charlie's voice hurtled him back to the present.

'With the right woman,' he said truthfully. He had thought the right woman didn't exist for him. His first marriage had been testament to that. Now the woman he wished could be *the right woman* had made it perfectly clear she didn't want anything more than this weekend.

'I hope you meet her then.'

He watched as she pushed away from the side of the pool, once again swimming on her back, exposing her pert breasts to him. The water sparkled under the sun but it couldn't detract from the beauty of her naked body as she swam. He was beginning to think he had.

'Are you ever going to come out of that pool?' Desperate to change the subject, he stood and picked up a towel. 'You'll be a mermaid before long.'

She laughed and swam to the steps at the far end of the pool, her slim figure clearly visible in the water, unleashing coils of lust within him. Lust. That was all this was—all it could be. He had to keep that at the forefront of his mind when dreams he'd long since hidden away threatened to reappear.

'I'm not mermaid material.' Slowly, as if aware of his eyes on her, aware of the hot lust she evoked within him, she climbed up the steps. Water rushed off her skin as she stood at the edge of the pool, pulling her hands down her hair, scrunching it into a ponytail to wring the water from it.

He couldn't move, couldn't take his eyes off her. Rivulets of water rushed over her breasts, down her stomach, and he fought hard against the urge to carry her back to his bed. She was so beautiful as she stood like a nymph with the morning sun glistening on her wet skin. It was like watching a film play out in slow motion as she walked towards him. Her angelic beauty stunned him into silence.

Unaware of what he was doing, he walked towards her and wrapped the towel around her, pulling her close against his now dry skin, relishing the wetness of hers. His gaze met hers, her green eyes heavy with unguarded passion that made his heart thud.

She reached up and brushed her lips over his and he closed his eyes as an intensity pressed down on his heart. Would he ever get enough of her? He knew the answer to that as her arms reached around his back, locking them together. No, he never would. She deepened the kiss, sending heat and need rushing through him again.

'We should take this inside,' he ground out as she pulled back and looked up at him. Her smile told him she knew exactly what she did to him and fully intended to continue the teasing she'd started as soon as she'd woken this morning.

'Yes,' she whispered. 'One last time.'

'One last time.' He repeated her words and kissed her, drinking her in, wanting more than one last time, but she hadn't set the boundaries for their weekend—he had and now he couldn't take this any further. He was already guilty enough of abusing the trust Seb had placed in him. As soon as they returned to Milan he had to put their relationship back where it belonged. On a professional level.

She pulled back from him and clutched the towel around her shoulders, although it didn't hide her luscious body completely from his view. With a coquettish little smile she took his hand and led him back up the stone steps and into the bedroom.

The sun now poured into the room, its rays falling onto the bed he'd hastily left after he'd heard her splash into the pool. The cream covers strewn aside, evidence of the hot hours they'd spent there last night.

She dropped the towel as she walked towards him, the makeshift ponytail hanging over one breast sending a rivulet of water down her sexy body. He took in a deep breath, savouring every last detail about her. Her impatience was clear as she closed the distance between them.

Before he knew what had happened she was in his arms, her body pressed hard against his, the torment of her nakedness too much. With an urgency he'd never experienced he lifted her from the wooden floor, her legs wrapping around him, only his trunks between them.

He carried her towards the bed, the heat of her against his arousal almost too much. Gently he lowered her onto the bed, watching as she slithered up towards the pillows. He crawled up the bed after her, his heart pounding in his chest so hard she must hear it. He wanted her so very much and intended to make the most of these last moments as lovers.

With frantic moves he tugged his trunks down, kicking them away as his gaze held hers, then took one slender ankle in his grasp and pulled her slowly back towards him. Her eyes flew wide but her heavy breaths, which made her breasts rise and fall provocatively, drove him on.

He moved over her, wanting to be deep inside her, to make her his one last time. He should be taking it slow but he couldn't hold back any longer.

'Sandro, stop.' She pushed against his chest, the urgency in her voice breaking the mind-numbing lust which robbed him of all coherent thought. 'We need protection.'

'*Maledizione.*' He shook with the effort of regaining control and looked at her face. With her eyes so wide and so green, all he could do was lower his head and kiss her. 'Forgive me.'

He didn't recognise the hoarse voice that had said those words. Never had he lost control quite so spectacularly and somewhere deep inside he was thankful that at least one of them had retained some sense.

He reached across to the bedside table and grabbed the box of condoms, tipping the last one out. Her words of moments ago floated back to him. *One last time.* He pushed the thought roughly aside as he rolled the protection on.

'Sorry,' she said shyly. 'But we don't want any consequences from this weekend.'

He looked at her, realisation hitting him. There were already consequences from this weekend, though not in the form of pregnancy. The consequences for him were that he'd unwittingly given his heart away, fallen for a woman he shouldn't even have had an affair with, let alone love.

'You're right, *mia cara.* There cannot be any consequences.'

She kissed him gently, her lips so light and teasing, sending him almost over the edge. 'None at all.' Her words whispered against his lips and he pushed all other thoughts from his mind until he couldn't hold back any longer.

'No,' he ground out as she pulled him towards her, wrapping her legs about him, taking him deep inside her. For the last time he made her his, the passion all-consuming.

His release was swift and she clung to him as he buried his head in her damp hair. '*Il mio amore*,' he murmured softly in Italian as he kissed her neck, not knowing what he was saying, his thoughts translating to words involuntarily as passion took over.

Was it his way of saying goodbye? He didn't know, but was grateful the words of love he'd voiced in his language hadn't appeared to have been understood, or even heard.

Charlie smoothed down the white dress she'd arrived in yesterday and glanced around the room one last time, not sure if she was checking for forgotten items or committing it to memory. Both, she told herself, because there wouldn't be any coming back. It was over. In just two more days she'd be back in England, back to her life. The moments of passion they'd shared would be locked away for good.

She walked around the room, her sandals tapping slowly on the wooden floor. She could still hear the soft words of Italian Sandro had spoken as they'd made love that one last time. She hadn't understood much of it, but one phrase now replayed over and over in her head.

Il mio *amore.*

My love.

She shook her head in denial. It must have been in the heat of the moment, something he said to every woman he made love to and nothing more. She clung to this idea, knowing she didn't want it to be anything more. Especially not from Alessandro.

They might have put aside their differences for a weekend of passion, enabling them to explore the explosive attraction that had been present from the very beginning, but as soon as they returned to Milan those differences would return. They would engulf them and mock her for her weakness at giving in to lust, because lust was all it was, all it ever could be.

As she thought of returning to Milan, she knew that, deep down, she could never forgive him for failing to ensure that the prototype that Seb had crashed that night was fit to drive. Their differences encroached like a menacing shadow. What had she done? Not only had she slept with the man responsible for Seb's death, but had enjoyed a whirlwind affair. One that had jumbled her emotions and tied her in knots.

Quickly she grabbed her bag and left the

room, not daring to look again at the bed which had been the focal point of so much pleasure, so much passion. She should be ashamed of herself. And, deep down, she was, but at least she'd got it out of her system, cleansed away the irrational desire she'd felt for him the instant her eyes had met his. There wouldn't be any *what ifs* when she returned home. But there would be recriminations.

Her heels clipped down the marble stairs, echoing around the vast hallway, and she paused as she saw Alessandro stood by the door, keys in hand, looking as desperate to get back to normal as she was.

Despite her bravado and knowing this was how it should be, her heart sank. If things had been different, if she didn't hold him responsible for Seb's accident, would they have been leaving as lovers too? She swallowed down the thought, straightened her shoulders and met his gaze head-on.

'It is time to go, no?' Her step faltered briefly at his heavily accented question, or was it a statement? Whatever it was, it was right. It was time to go, time to leave their passion within the luxury of this villa.

'It is,' she said and continued down the stairs, her chin held high. 'Time to get back to reality.'

CHAPTER TEN

CHARLIE HAD NEVER been so tense. The drive back to Milan had been almost silent, with the exception of a few attempts at polite conversation which had withered like flowers in parched earth.

She followed Alessandro into the apartment, trying not to notice the masculine scent of his aftershave, which trailed tantalisingly in his wake. She might have decided to distance herself from him but her body was having a hard time accepting it.

'I will book into a hotel, if you can recommend one close by.' She forced the words out, knowing it would be for the best. What they'd shared over the weekend had no place in the present and certainly not the future. She'd made it very clear to him she wasn't looking for more than a passing distraction and he'd made it easy, setting the time limit and taking her away.

But now they were back in Milan. Back with their problems. All she wanted was to get through the next two days and leave—but not until she'd found what she'd come to Italy for. Answers.

He turned to face her, his expression set in a hard mask, his eyes unreadable. 'That will not be necessary. The room you occupied on the first night is ready for you.'

Her room was ready for her. Didn't that tell her enough? He'd obviously instructed his housekeeper to put the few things she'd left behind back in the room Seb had once used, effectively removing her presence as a lover from his apartment. It was what she wanted, what she needed, so why did it hurt so much?

'Under the circumstances, it would be best if I stayed in a hotel.' She forced herself to believe her words. After all, she had little hope of him doing so if she didn't.

'No.' The word snapped from him as he tossed his car keys onto the marble worktop of the kitchen in an irritated fashion. 'The circumstances, as you so nicely put it, are that we are back after a weekend away. Our weekend of fun is over. It was not a for ever arrangement and nothing more than an affair.'

'All the more reason I stay in a hotel, don't you think?'

He looked at her sternly and the hard businessman he was showed through. 'You said it wasn't for ever, so why do you need to leave? The weekend affair we agreed on is over, now it is back to business.'

'Very well,' she relented, but knew she had to go back to England sooner than originally planned. Once their meeting at the test track was over tomorrow she would be on the next plane home. She'd walk out right now, if only she had the answers she needed.

Resigned to staying in his apartment one more night, she walked over to the windows, looking out at the Duomo. When she'd first arrived its magnificence had captured her imagination, now she just looked blankly at it. So much had changed in just two days, but each mile they'd driven on their way back to Milan had wiped out their weekend, kiss by kiss. They were back where they had started, but the simmer of sexual tension was now tinged with regret. At least for her it was; for Alessandro it had been replaced by indifference.

With a small sigh she turned and absently looked at the newspaper neatly placed on the ornate desk which occupied the corner of the living area. Already a photograph of her and Alessandro arriving at the launch party had a front-page position. The few words written beneath were incomprehensible and she turned the page. Maybe more of the launch would be on another page.

She froze.

The image which leapt to life from the page scorched her with hot memories. She and Alessandro were there, in the paper. Not the happy smiles of their arrival, but the passionate kiss against the car. The kiss that had happened after everyone had left.

She looked down at the picture, which sparked with passion, showing lovers locked in their own world, oblivious to everything, even the intrusion of the photographer. When and how had this been taken? Then her body chilled. Had Alessandro known of this? She recalled his intent as he'd taken her in his arms, the way he'd rendered all thought impossible as his lips had claimed hers.

He hadn't kissed her because he'd wanted to, because he'd been unable to resist, but to set up the perfect photo opportunity. One that would show to the world he wasn't in any way to blame for Seb's accident, that she and her family had more than given their stamp of approval to a car which had taken the life of a young driver.

'Did you know about this?' She closed the

paper, unable to look at the sizzling photograph a moment longer. He approached the table, a frown on his face, and she looked up at him, hostility masking her shock.

'*Sì*. It is what I requested.' His calm words did little to soothe her jangled nerves. So he had set her up, used her like a pawn in his game. Not only did her presence at the launch suggest she didn't blame him or the Roselli company, it showed an intimate moment she had no wish for the world to see.

She blinked in surprise. 'What you requested?'

'Come, Charlotte—' his accent lavished her full name as he looked down at her, having glanced briefly at the paper '—a front-page photograph of us together is exactly the sort of advertisement I'd hoped for. You brought glamour and style to the occasion and, of course, your family's blessing.'

'What about this?' Furiously she dashed back the front page and watched as he looked down at the photo of their passionately hot kiss. 'Did you request this?'

He scanned the words beneath the photo, words she didn't understand. His silence was almost too much as he placed one palm on the desk, leaning down to read. The suspense of what it all meant was wrapping up with her initial anger until she thought she might explode. 'Did you?'

'No.' He shook his head, continuing to study the piece. 'Not this.'

'What does it say?' Anger overtook the suspense, filling her mind and her body. He'd set her up. He'd used her. Had that been his intention even as he'd entered her home and tried to convince her to go to Milan? She swallowed down the sour taste of deceit, determined not to let her feelings out. She had to remain calm.

He turned to look at her, his eyes locking with hers, but the brown of his were devoid of any emotion and her stomach lurched sickeningly. What had she done—to herself and to Seb? She'd sullied Seb's memory and her reputation into the bargain, falling into the worst trap imaginable.

Alessandro looked into the confusion of her eyes and tried to push back all the guilt he'd so far managed to keep at bay. She was angry, there wasn't any denying that, but she also looked scared and he didn't blame her.

'It says your passion shows your approval of the car which claimed the life of your brother.' He didn't translate word for word what had been written beneath that blisteringly hot photograph. He didn't think her anger would allow him enough time, so quickly he'd summed it up, leaving her to draw her own conclusions.

'What's next, Sandro? A photo of me, naked in your pool?' The accusation in her voice cut hard and deep. Did she really think he was that callous?

What could he say? This photograph alone went against everything he'd said to her that day in her cottage. He'd persuaded her to come to the launch in Milan, telling her Seb had wanted it. Now, thanks to a rogue photographer, something he would swiftly sort out, she thought he'd set her up.

'That will not be possible. You would not have been seen by anyone.' He pushed the image of her swimming naked aside. Now was not the time for such heated recollections.

'Damn you, Alessandro. You tricked me into swimming with nothing on, even had the nerve to come out in your trunks. What will the next headline say?' Her eyes were sharp, her expression strained as she pressed her lips tightly together, expectantly waiting for his answer.

He clenched his fists against the urge to hold her, pull her towards him and calm her. Instinctively he knew that would be the worst possible thing to do. She was pushing him further away, something he was certain she would have done even without the help of the newspaper report.

He glowered at her, his pulse racing erratically. 'I did not trick you at all. Your swim this morning will remain between us.'

'I don't believe you.' The words fired from her like bullets and she stepped closer to him, chin lifted and standing so tall with indignation he would hardly have had to lower his head to kiss her lips. The temptation was great, but he resisted.

'Have I lied to you, *cara*?'

Of course he'd lied to her. From the night of the accident and the moment he'd discovered the truth, the real reason Seb had crashed, he'd been lying to her. But they were lies to protect her and Seb, to keep the Warrington name out of the papers. They were lies he had to continue with. He'd made a promise, first to Seb, then to her father and he would keep both of those promises. He was a man of honour, whatever the cost.

'If you can set up publicity like this—' she flicked the paper, not taking her eyes from him '—then you are capable of anything, any lie, just to get what you want.'

He shook his head slowly, admiring the fire of anger emanating from her, not wanting to dampen the passion. But her passion was something he could no longer have; there were too many secrets, too many lies between them.

She made a sound that was like a growl and put her hands to her face, fingers splayed over her eyes. Then she dropped her hands, letting them fall with a slap against her as exasperation got the better of her. 'I was stupid ever to have believed you—or trusted you.'

He shook his head and reached for her, desperate to offer some comfort at least. She flinched, stepping back out of his reach.

Her eyes, angry and glittering, searched his face, finally narrowing in suspicion. 'You've done nothing but lie to me, Sandro; since the moment you arrived at my cottage it's been nothing but lies.'

'*Dio mio!* How can you say that?' Exasperation coursed through him and he pushed his fingers through his hair, unable to comprehend the circles she was spinning around him. Circles that made the temptation to tell the truth almost too much.

'Because of this.' She snatched the paper from the desk, shaking it in front of him. 'You used me. This has nothing at all to do with Seb. You're just trying to ease your conscience, ease your guilt over the accident.'

'My conscience is clear, Charlie.' It was—he was doing this for Seb.

'Charlotte.' Her voice cracked like a whip as she corrected his use of her name, glaring up at him. 'And once again you are lying. I don't believe Seb really asked for me to be at the launch. It was you who wanted me there all along; you were just preying on my emotions.'

'Seb did ask for you to be there; that much is true.' Her anger lacerated him but he stood firm against it, holding the truth inside.

'That much? So you are lying about something?' Her voice lowered in suspicion and she looked at him through narrowing eyes.

He had to think fast, keep ahead of her suspicions. 'I have not lied, but certain things need to remain out of the limelight.'

'Like this?' She stabbed at the photo of them kissing and inwardly he breathed a sigh of relief. He'd almost blown it, almost revealed there were things he was holding back on. Her anger fizzed around him, preventing her from thinking in any rational kind of way.

Charlie couldn't take any more and tossed the offending newspaper back onto the desk, glaring angrily at the man she'd been stupid enough to fall in love with.

Fall in love?

Panic rushed through her faster than any car she'd ever driven. She couldn't love him. Not Alessandro Roselli. Not the man she blamed for Seb's accident and the man who had cruelly tricked her and used her emotional weakness for his own ends.

'You can't run and hide from this, Charlotte.' Alessandro's words filtered through the hazy fog of anger and shock that obscured just about everything. Hadn't he used that phrase earlier? Then he'd been referring to love. Now it was truth. She sensed he was keeping something from her—and she was sure it wasn't love, despite his murmured words of endearment just hours ago.

'I don't run.' She stood in the doorway of the room she'd used the first night at his apartment, swallowing down the bitter taste of reality, refusing to admit any such thing to him.

'Then what are you doing now, *cara*?' His words were softer, coaxing and cajoling. She was running, she was hiding; they both knew it, but she'd never admit it to him. Especially as it was love she was running from. She had no choice. This man didn't love her and never would. He'd agreed to the weekend affair for exactly the same reasons as she had. He didn't do love.

'I'm not the only one running or hiding, Alessandro.' She spoke calmly even though her heart was thudding painfully in her chest and her knees were suddenly weak.

His eyes narrowed in suspicion. 'What is it you want to say, Charlotte?'

She ignored the way he used her name, the way his accent caressed it, keeping herself focused on what she really wanted. 'You are hiding the truth of Seb's accident.'

'I've told you all there is to tell,' he said, his eyes searching her face.

'We both know that's not exactly true.' She lifted her chin in a show of defiance, looked him in the eye and continued. 'You told me what you want me to know.'

'It wasn't the car, Charlotte.'

'So it was the driver. It was Seb.' She wasn't about to let this go now. Whatever the truth was, she had to know.

'It was. I'm sorry.' He reached out to her but she flinched.

'Don't.' The word was spat out as she battled with the idea that the accident had possibly been Seb's fault and that Alessandro, for whatever reason, wasn't going to tell her.

'You should talk to your father,' he said quietly, seemingly indifferent to her anger.

'I intend to. Right now.' She turned and

moved into her room, purposefully keeping the door open. She wanted him to see her ring her father, watch whilst she asked for the full facts.

Angrily grabbing her phone from her bag, she dialled the number. It rang out before going to answerphone. But she wasn't beaten yet. 'If you will excuse me,' she said tartly as she began to shut the door, 'I have packing to do.'

With that she turned her back on him, resolutely shutting the door behind her. She dropped to sit on the bed, all the fight deflating from her. Outside, a nearby bell tower chimed the hour and she fought against threatening tears.

It was time to go home. Time to go back to her life and pick up the pieces that had been discarded the day she'd heard that her beloved brother had died. Just as her father had been trying to persuade her to do for many months. But she was sure he wouldn't have wanted her to fall in love with Alessandro Roselli and that was just what she'd done.

She thought of her mother, but she dismissed the idea of confiding in her. She was always too willing to blame the racing world for bringing her family down and tearing it apart. It would only give more weight to her argument against the whole lifestyle.

Resigned to the pain that Alessandro's betrayal had brought, she pulled out her tablet and searched for London-bound flights, booking on one the next evening. At least that would give her time to go back to the test track in the morning. She had one last thing to do before she went.

Then it would be goodbye and this time she meant it to be for ever.

Alessandro had watched her walk away, desperate to call her name, to make her turn and look at him. But it wouldn't do any good. They should never have become lovers and they could never be together. The hours they'd shared at his villa must be forgotten and he hoped they hadn't been tailed by any more photographers. It was bad enough her father might see the one of them kissing, but what if he saw her, cares cast aside, enjoying time with him? Not that they'd be shots of her at his pool—security was good at the villa—but they'd spent a lot of time out and about, doing tourist things.

She had paused in the doorway and turned to look at him, her green eyes large and full of sadness, and as they met his he'd felt the disappointment crash over him like a stormy sea.

'Goodnight, Alessandro.' Her voice had lost the anger and hard edge of earlier but he remained where he was, rooted to the marble floor, unable to decide what course of action was best.

'*Buonanotte*, Charlotte.' He couldn't stand and watch her any more, not if he wanted to keep his distance, so he turned and marched off to his study, a place he could lose himself in work. Behind him, he heard the bedroom door click softly shut but it sounded loud and piercing in his head, like a gunshot.

He didn't sit at his desk, didn't open his laptop and work. He couldn't. His mind was going over every single detail of the last few days. From the moment he'd seen her working in her garden to the hot passionate nights they'd shared.

What was the matter with him? He couldn't want her, couldn't have her, but he did. He wanted to wake up with her each and every day. He paced the room, stopping to look out across the rooftops of Milan as the sun slipped lower in the sky, casting its orange glow onto the old buildings.

When he'd promised Seb he'd look after her as if she was his own sister he had never imagined it would be so difficult. What would he do if the situation was reversed, if it was his sister involved with a man who would break her heart?

He clenched his hands into tight fists, the thought of anyone hurting or taking advantage of his sister filling him with rage like an aggressive and territorial lion. Yet that was what he'd done. He'd gone back on his promise to Seb, just by kissing Charlie and by taking her away to explore the passion that had sparked to life the instant they'd met—he hadn't looked after her, as he'd promised her father he would.

The only thing he had been able to do right was keep the truth from her and even the success of that seemed in doubt as she probed into every drawing and detail Seb had made, and asked the manufacturing team pointed questions about whether certain design developments had been made before or after the accident.

He closed his eyes and memories of the day Seb had told him the truth descended. He could still hear Seb, his voice weak as he lay in the hospital bed, begging him to keep the drink and drug problem from his sister.

Please, Sandro, don't tell her. It will break her heart. Whatever else you do, don't tell her.

Seb's words came back to him, as clear as if he was at his side again. Alessandro rubbed his hands together, the light pressure of Seb's grasp once again on his hands, and in his mind he could see Seb's face, so like Charlie's, begging him to keep his secret.

Had he known then he wasn't going to make it?

With a furious curse, Alessandro strode back out of his office. He couldn't let Charlie sit there alone, worrying about everything. Outside her door, he paused. Was he doing the right thing? He was normally so decisive, so sure of what needed to be done, but where this woman was concerned he was the opposite.

He knocked on the door and almost instantly it was opened. 'You can't stay in there all night.' He attempted light-hearted chatter, something she'd proved to be very good at over the weekend. The frosty glare she sent him told him that he hadn't yet mastered that art.

'We could go out for dinner.' He didn't like her silence, as cold as her eyes, and he had the feeling he was in ever-deepening quicksand.

She raised a haughty brow at him. 'So you can set me up again, get yet another photo of us together?'

'Charlotte…' He stepped closer but she moved back, using the door as a shield.

'No, Sandro. I'm not prepared to take the risk. We should never have spent the weekend together.' She moved further behind the door. Hiding from him, from what they'd shared.

She was right and he moved away, not missing the relief on her face. 'I knew nothing about that photograph and I'm sorry it has upset you.'

'Please, I don't want to talk about it now.' Her green eyes looked moist and guilt tugged at him. He wasn't doing a very good job of looking after her at all.

He nodded his acceptance of her reason, knowing he was only making the whole situation worse. 'I will find whoever it was who took the photo and personally deal with him.'

'It won't take away the fact that you used me and Seb to promote the car, to clear its reputation and your name.'

'I have no need to clear my name, Charlotte.'

'You do to me.' Those words stung him as they hit home and finally his business sense returned. He needed to step back, assess the situation and plan his next move.

'Very well, I will.' He walked away, not stopping to see how his words had been received. If she wanted proof he'd find it, but how could he do so without giving away Seb's secret—or his true feelings for her?

CHAPTER ELEVEN

CHARLIE HAD SECRETLY hoped Alessandro would have gone to wherever it was he went that first night, but as she'd emerged from her room earlier that morning he'd been preparing coffee, looking so handsome she'd actually stopped to take in every detail, from his expensive charcoal suit to the shiny black shoes.

Now, enclosed in his car, painfully aware of every move he made as he drove, she wished she'd taken the early morning flight to London. Instead, she'd been lured by the opportunity to be at the test track again, hoping she would find out what Alessandro was keeping from her about Seb's accident. Because something was, of that she was certain.

'I have a meeting at lunchtime.' His accented voice jolted her from her thoughts as they drove. She wanted to look at him, savour his handsome profile, but couldn't allow herself to. She'd imprinted more than enough images into her mind during their weekend. It was time to stop, to let go of something that could never be and should never have happened.

'I need to be at the airport this evening, so I will arrange a taxi.' Her words, though flowing and easy, didn't feel it. She was sure it sounded as if she was stumbling over each one and she ran her fingers through her hair nervously.

He turned to look at her just at the moment she gave in to temptation to look at him and for a split second their gazes met, then he focused back on the road as they turned into the test track.

'You said you weren't running.' His voice was deep and stern, but she fixed her attention on the workshops as he pulled up and parked. The engine fell silent and her heartbeat thumped so loudly she was sure he would hear it.

'I'm not running.' The angry words flew from her before she had time to think. 'I'm going back to my life, to the things I did before Seb's accident. It's what he would have wanted. The only good thing that has come out of this visit.'

She got out of the car, anxious to put some distance between herself and Alessandro. It didn't matter how much her body craved his, she had to remember what he'd done, how he'd manipulated her to get what he wanted in an attempt to assuage his guilt and clear his name.

She all but marched off towards the workshops, hearing the driver's door shut behind her then feeling his presence closing the distance as he caught up with her. Her pulse leapt as she reached the door but, before she could do anything, he pressed his palm against it, preventing her from opening it, stopping her from escaping him.

'That is all? There must be something else you want to accuse me of?' His voice deepened and she raised her eyes to meet his, determined not to let him know how much he affected her.

'"Something else" being the fact that you virtually sold me to the press for your own gain?' She hurled the words at him, indignation spiking her into action. 'Or is it the fact that you seduced me? You let me believe I was doing all this for Seb, when it wasn't. It was for you.'

His brows lifted suggestively, his expression of smug satisfaction almost too much to tolerate. 'As I recall, *cara*, it was you who seduced me.'

She clenched her hands into tight fists, digging her nails into her palms. Pain made her gasp, emotional and physical pain. It was just what she needed to remind her of what was at stake. Not only her brother's good name and her reputation, but her heart.

'Don't flatter yourself. What I did, I did for Seb.' She flung the first words that came to mind at him, then bit down on any more. She didn't want to let him know how much she was hurting, how hard she had fallen for him. He must never know. It would give him the trump card.

'Not because you wanted to, because you couldn't resist the fire that leapt to life between us the moment we met?' He loomed over her, trapping her and forcing her to confront this.

'Okay. So I couldn't resist the *fire*, as you put it. But that fire is well and truly out now.' She pushed his hand aside and opened the door, thankful to see mechanics and drivers busy at work. He'd never pursue her now, not so publicly.

Behind her, she heard him talking rapidly in Italian, heard his footsteps as he marched across the spotless floor of the workshop. She had no idea what he was saying, but it seemed that everyone was ready to do as he asked, waiting for their instruction.

At a loss as to just what she should do now they were here again and with so many curious glances her way, she went over to a car she hadn't seen here last time. Obviously it was a new prototype for yet another road sports car. The black paintwork shone beneath the bright lights of the workshop and the elegant curves of the wing of the car caught her eye. It was very different from the flashy red one her brother had played a part in. That had been exactly what she would have expected from Seb.

This had more style, as if designed for speed and comfort. The grille at the front was far more sedate, more classical and looked much less aggressive than Seb's. It was still low and sporty, its power subtly evident, but with a sophistication that made her immediately think of Alessandro. Was this car all his work?

As he spoke to his team, Alessandro watched Charlie walking towards the car. He saw her head tilt to one side in contemplation as she stood by the front wing, looking along the line of the car. He could almost hear her mind working, assessing the car's capabilities.

With a few final instructions, he left his team and walked over to where Charlie was now looking inside the latest prototype. This was his design; everything he'd ever wanted in a car was going into it.

'This looks like it has the potential to be a car in a league of its own.' Her voice oozed enthusiasm that no amount of animosity between them could disguise. 'Who designed it?'

He wasn't about to tell her it was his work, not so soon after the launch of Seb's car. He'd never intended for her to see it, worried she'd think he'd moved onto a new project before Seb's car had even been launched. 'A team effort.'

'A good one,' she said, running her fingers along it, just as she had done with the first car. 'A really good one. Black suits it.'

He couldn't listen to her praise for his work, even if she didn't know it as such. This was the woman he'd done nothing but try to protect, the woman who heated his blood, making him want her more than any other. Now she hated him and was about to walk out of his life. But he couldn't stop her.

'I have arranged for Giovanni to take you back to the apartment to collect your belongings and then on to the airport.' He had to keep the conversation on neutral territory. If she continued to talk about the car, he knew his passion for it would show, just as his passion for her could so easily come out.

'Yes, of course, thank you.' Her curt tone reminded him of her earlier anger and he knew he was doing the right thing. If he stayed any longer he would tell her anything to disperse that anger which hovered around them and relight the passion they'd shared at the weekend.

The best thing he could do was go. Walk away and never look back.

'*Arrivederci*, Charlotte.'

Before he lost control of his emotions he stalked from the workshop, his footsteps echoing loudly across the floor. He could feel her eyes on him, feel the intensity of her gaze, and he reminded himself of her warning that first night they'd spent together.

I don't do for ever.

Audaciously, he'd echoed her warning, using his first marriage to back up the claim, but had he really meant it? At that moment he had, but now, as he strode out of her life for ever, he knew that it was no longer true. He wanted for ever and he was turning his back on the one woman he wanted. Truly wanted.

As the sunlight dazzled him and the door

shut behind him he knew it was over. Whatever it was between them, it was gone. All that was left was his one-sided desire for a woman who thought he'd set her up and who held him responsible for her brother's accident.

This really was goodbye.

He got into his car and reversed hastily backwards, tyres squealing in protest, then he sped off, wanting only to get as far away from her as possible. The sooner she returned to England, the better.

Embarrassment washed over Charlie as she suddenly became aware of someone standing at her side. She was still looking at the closed door, could still hear the screech of tyres that suggested Alessandro couldn't get away fast enough.

'*Scuzi,*' the man at her side said; thankfully, he seemed unaware of her emotional turmoil. 'We will leave for Milan in one hour, but you may wait in Signor Roselli's office.'

She smiled at his heavily accented English, as appealing as Sandro's, but it didn't have the same effect on her. It didn't melt her from the inside, making her want to close her eyes as he spoke. 'Thank you; I will be ready.'

She turned and walked to the office, nerves cascading over her. This was the one place she hadn't been able to look for evidence of Alessandro's guilt. Was this where she could find out the secret he was keeping?

She opened the door and immediately felt Alessandro's presence. How could he affect her so, even when he wasn't anywhere near her? She took a gulp of air into her lungs, focusing on what she'd come to Italy for in the first place. Proof of who was to blame for her brother's death.

She sat in the chair at his desk, unable to shake the feeling of unease, and glanced out at the workshop to see the team working on other cars. Her presence at Alessandro's desk didn't seem to worry them and she relaxed a bit.

At first she flicked through some design drawings, spread out and pushed to one side, then turned her attention to the files on the shelf above the desk. One stood out, as if calling for her attention, and she reached for it, feeling more and more like a spy.

The first few sections held nothing but engine reports but, as she flicked through the file, one unmarked section at the back caught her attention. She opened the page and looked at the photo of the car, a grey prototype the same as she'd driven, its specification listed below. With trembling fingers she turned the page.

Accident Report.

The words rushed at her and her stomach lurched sickeningly. She blinked, as if doing so would erase the truth that was set out in black and white before her.

'Oh, Seb,' she whispered and closed her eyes, but the words were imprinted there already. 'Why didn't you tell me?'

The question bounced around the office and she glanced at the team beyond the window, sure they would have heard it. Satisfied they hadn't, she looked back at the page, the words still a shock.

'Driver error.' She whispered the words, then paused before continuing. 'The driver was found to have significant levels of alcohol and drugs in his system.'

She leant her elbows on the desk and pressed her hands against her face. Could this be true? Could she believe it? She read the rest of the report, each point stating the car was in good working order.

With a heavy heart she closed the file and pushed it away from her, not wanting to read another word of it and wishing Alessandro was here to explain why he was using her brother as a scapegoat.

Alessandro had already shown how calculating he could be with the photo of the launch. Had this accident report been fabricated too?

The man she'd spoken to earlier knocked on the office door, dragging her from her thoughts. 'Now we shall leave.' He'd discarded his overalls and was every inch the Italian in his jeans and leather jacket, but he was far from the Italian she really wanted. The one she hated and loved.

Did that mean it wasn't hate? Or did it mean it wasn't love? Two powerfully strong emotions and they were tearing her apart. So what did she want it to be? Hate would mean staying in the past, never moving on, and she couldn't do that any longer. Love would mean forgiveness.

She stood and smiled, pushing her jumbled thoughts about all she'd just read to the back of her mind. 'Yes, I have a plane to catch.'

'*Sì, sì,*' he said as he walked towards the same door Sandro had left from an hour earlier. Where was he now? In his meeting, not giving her a second thought? Or was he relieved she would now be about to leave Italy and his life?

She pondered those questions as the car left the test track and within a few minutes they were on the busy roads and heading back to Milan. Charlie sat in silence, watching the countryside flash past, so caught up in her emotions she didn't even give the car they were in any thought. Her mind was with the man she loved. A man she should never have fallen in love with.

'Goodbye is hard, no?' The driver spoke, dragging her from her despondent thoughts.

'Yes,' she said before she'd realised it, adding quickly, 'but only because it is also saying goodbye to my brother.'

She hadn't expected this personal conversation and was glad to see they had reached Milan. Very soon she would be on her own, which was what she craved more than anything right now.

Thankfully, the traffic congestion took the driver's attention away from the conversation and she smiled at his exasperated sighs as they negotiated the streets towards Alessandro's apartment.

'I will get a taxi from here,' she said as she got out of the car outside the old building that she still couldn't believe was home to such a modern and powerful man.

'No, my instruction was to bring you here,' he said as he pressed the required numbers into the keypad, obviously used to letting himself in. Was this Sandro's right-hand man? Could he tell her the truth about the accident report? 'Then we go to the airport.'

She sensed he wanted to deliver her to the airport as soon as possible. Maybe that would be for the best. Alessandro had obviously asked that she be escorted all the way, to ensure she had actually left. 'Thank you. I will only be a few minutes.'

The driver handed her a key and she rushed up the stairs, into the apartment, trying not to think of all that had happened there in such a short time. Not wanting to linger, she grabbed her already packed case and left. As she shut the door, she closed her eyes briefly, pushing memories of being with Sandro to the back of her mind. But it wasn't easy. Even though she knew she shouldn't, she loved him. How did you switch that off? Finally, she went back down to where the driver was waiting.

Moments later they were once again in the traffic, heading towards the airport. She kept her eyes firmly fixed ahead of her as she thought of all that had happened. Would Seb have approved of her and Sandro—would he have been happy they were together?

'Did you know my brother?' She asked the question casually. This would be the last chance she got to talk to anyone from the test track and she wasn't going to waste this opening, no matter how small.

'*Sì*, he was a good driver, a very good driver, but things got too much for him. We tried to help.' His attention was kept on the busy road, his words had been said in such a distracted way, he obviously hadn't thought about them.

So it *was* true. She tried hard to keep her voice normal when all she wanted to do was scream and shout, but she couldn't. It was obvious this man thought she knew all about it.

'I didn't realise you'd helped him too,' she said as calmly as possible, luring him into divulging more of the truth. Each word he said confirmed all she'd seen in the report.

'Alessandro helped most, but I was also there that night and it became my secret too.'

What kind of sister had she been, not to have noticed Seb's problems? Guilt spiked cruelly at her. Not a hint of what she'd read had reached the press. Part of her clung desperately to the hope that this was because it was all part of an elaborate fabrication by Alessandro. She didn't want to believe it of Seb; it was too painful.

'Sorry, I didn't mean to upset you,' he said and she opened her eyes to see him looking at her whilst they'd stopped at a red light.

'I do still find it upsetting, sorry.' She dabbed the corner of her eye with her finger-tips, glad when the lights changed and they moved off, taking his gaze from her. Did he know he'd walked into her trap?

'The airport,' Giovanni said as the terminal buildings came into view and the relief in his voice would have been comical if she hadn't been so strung out by his conversation.

He pulled into a space and got out, but she wasn't done yet. Whatever he knew, she had to find out. Good or bad, she just had to hear it. Could it be any worse than all she had just read?

'Please—' she put her hand on his arm, using all her feminine charm, bombarding him with questions. 'You said you were there too. How bad were Seb's problems? Did they really cause the accident?'

He looked at his watch. 'You will be late for your flight.'

'Please.'

He sighed and then put his hand over hers as it clutched at his arm. 'He'd been drinking heavily that day—and the drugs…' He shrugged, his face apologetic. 'They made him wild, irrational. We couldn't stop him.'

'We?' she whispered, scared to let go of his arm in case she fell to the floor with shock.

'*Sì*, Signor Roselli and myself. Of course, we said nothing after the accident that would blacken your brother's name.' He took her hand and held it between both of his and looked at her, genuine concern in his face. 'I thought you knew.'

'I did,' she bluffed, not wanting to tell him she'd only just discovered what now appeared to be the truth. 'It hurts to hear it again. I'm sorry.'

'Now you must go; you will be late for your plane.' The relief on his face only cemented the bad images of her brother, under the influence of drink and drugs, driving the car. How had she not known he had problems? How had he managed to hide it so well from her?

'Yes, my plane.' She forced the words out slowly. They sounded hollow to her ears, but she picked up her small case and walked away from this man and the truth that had shattered everything she'd held dear.

Once inside the building she ran to the Ladies, her insides churning alarmingly. She splashed cold water over her face, not caring about her make-up, just wanting to stave off the nausea. She looked at her reflection in the mirror, as if for reassurance.

Could it be true?

She didn't want it to be, but certain things

were slotting into place, suddenly becoming much clearer. Seb had dropped out of the final races of last year's season, claiming injury, but had dismissed it as they'd spoken on the phone, telling her to stop mothering him. Had he had a problem even then?

'No, it can't be true… Sandro would have said something.' She spoke aloud to her shocked reflection.

Then it hit her like a brick being hurled through the air. Alessandro Roselli had been covering for her brother, not to keep Seb's good name but to save his own damn reputation. To do that he'd dragged hers through the mire too. That photograph of them kissing backed it all up.

She pressed her palms to her face and took in a deep breath. There was only one person other than Alessandro who could confirm this.

Her father. He'd flown out to Italy as soon as news of the accident had reached them. Seb had died just hours after he'd arrived, but her father would know if drugs and alcohol had been the cause.

She frowned at herself in the mirror. Why hadn't he told her? Why had he kept it a secret and then still supported Alessandro? There was only one answer. It wasn't true and he knew nothing of the cover-up story that was being used. The report must be a cover-up. It had even been left in easy view, just waiting for her to find it.

Frantically she searched in her bag for her phone and with shaking fingers pressed call on her father's number.

'Hello, Charlie.' Her father sounded cautious and not his usual self.

'Is it true, Dad?' She didn't waste any time on pleasantries.

On the other end of the phone her father sighed, then horrifyingly she knew it was. She clutched the washbasin with her free hand, watching the colour drain from the shocked face with hollowed eyes which looked back at her from the mirror.

'Oh, Dad, why didn't you tell me?' She shook her head in disbelief, feeling ever more disconnected from the woman staring back at her in the mirror.

'You didn't need to know. Where are you, Charlie?' She could hear the restrained panic in her father's voice and her heart clenched.

'On my way home. We'll talk soon. I have to check in or I'll miss the flight.'

'Charlie?'

'Yes, Dad.'

'See you soon.'

Her heart constricted as if a snake were torturing her, squashing every last beat from her, and she couldn't say anything else. Instead she cut the connection before she cried, before she lost complete control. That was something she had to save until later. Much later. Right now she had a plane to catch.

CHAPTER TWELVE

ALESSANDRO STALKED AROUND the check-in desks, scanning the throng of passengers, but with each passing minute his impatience increased. Where was she? He still didn't want to accept what had drawn him to the airport instead of his meeting, but when the call from Giovanni had come through he'd been glad he was only minutes away. He couldn't let her leave without talking to her, checking she was all right.

The queue for the London flight was diminishing fast and his agitation increased. Giovanni had told him she'd acted as if she'd known everything. But how? He stalked over to the desk again, the operator who'd denied him passenger information earlier giving him a suspicious look.

Maledizione! Where was she? It was as if she'd just vanished. That or she'd got through security so quickly because she hated him. He didn't blame her. He hated himself right now. He should have found a way to tell her, found a way around the promise he'd made to Seb and her father. Hadn't he done just that so he could have a weekend affair with her? So why hadn't he been able to do the same with the truth of the accident?

Angrily he stabbed his fingers through his hair and marched away from the check-in desk. Even his charm had deserted him as he'd tried to find out if Charlie had checked in or even what flight she had booked. Now what? Book on the next flight to England?

Suddenly his attention was caught as he saw a woman hurriedly leaving the terminal building and quickly he raced after her. His heart beat like a drum with the hope that it was Charlie, that she'd changed her mind, but once outside in the evening sunlight he couldn't see her. Taxis pulled away in rapid succession. He had no idea if she was in one—or if it had been her.

More deflated than he'd ever been in his adult life, he stood as everyone bustled past him, hurrying to or from the airport, all seemingly happy. The roar of jet engines as they soared into the sky sounded like a death knell. Each time he heard one, his heart died a bit more. She could be on board.

But what if she wasn't?

What if the woman he'd seen, the one he'd wanted to be Charlie, was her? Where would she go?

Realisation hit him. There was only one place she'd go to be alone with memories of her brother. One place she'd be sure he or his staff wouldn't be. But should he go there and disturb her?

The answer was simple. He had to. He had to find her and tell her everything, explain why he'd kept the secret. She already hated him. He didn't have anything to lose. He'd rather she hurled accusations at him than disappear with a revelation like that on her mind. Purposefully, he strode back to the car park and set about the tedious task of negotiating Milan's traffic.

The drive to the hotel proved almost impossible as a minor bump had closed the most direct route, forcing him down narrow side streets and testing his patience to the full. All the while he imagined her there, with the car that had been at the launch, alone and hurting. Hurt he'd caused.

With a big sigh of relief he pulled up at the hotel, jumped from the car, tossed the keys at the doorman for parking and went through the revolving doors. Slowly he made his way towards the room that had become a temporary showroom for the sleek red beast that had consumed Seb so utterly. Benign and innocuously it sat there, its secrets hidden within its beauty. The silence of the room hit him. Quickly he looked around, but couldn't see her.

Then a small movement caught his attention at the far end of the room. She was there, sitting at a table with her back to him. Relief rushed through him at top speed. Cautiously he moved towards her.

Charlie sat, totally lost in thought, the feeling of betrayal stinging more than a swarm of bees could. The two men she loved had betrayed her. She looked down at the cup of coffee, now very cold, as if it could answer her problems, tell her what to do.

Why had she come here? Why hadn't she just got on the plane and left? Because she needed answers and she couldn't go anywhere until she got them. The only problem was that Alessandro held those answers—and he'd just driven away from her at top speed.

With a sigh she looked at the sleek red car. The secrets locked within it had only just started to slip from its powerful clutches.

'Why, Seb?' She whispered the question

aloud but silence came back at her, a painful echo.

Suddenly a sizzling sensation hurtled down her spine and she knew she wasn't alone. There was only one person who had that effect on her. The man she hated and loved with equal passion. Alessandro Roselli.

'Haven't you done enough damage already?' The venomous tone of her words surprised her as much as him, but she kept her back to him, looking resolutely at the car.

'I did what I had to.' He came to stand beside her but still she didn't look at him.

'Of course you did.' The crispness of each word was colder than a frosty morning. 'You did exactly what you needed to do to keep your name from being dragged through the dirt.'

'You've got it all wrong, Charlie.'

'Charlotte,' she snapped and looked up at him, confused by the anger and the raw betrayal which filled her. 'And I haven't got it wrong at all.'

'It isn't what you think.' He moved to stand in front of her, obscuring her view of the car, her link to her brother.

She stood up and moved past him, towards the car, anything other than stay beneath his intense gaze. 'So you deny you brought me here under the pretence it was what Seb wanted, seduced me so that you could get the ultimate photograph for the press and then keep the truth of Seb's problems from me.'

'I never meant to hurt you, Charlie.'

'Charlotte!' She whirled round and stood to face him, catching her breath at the hard look in his eyes. Where had the loving man she'd spent the weekend with gone—or was that also part of his game plan?

'I can see you aren't prepared to listen to anything I have to say.' He sat down in the chair she'd just vacated but couldn't disguise the tension and irritation in his body.

'Too right I'm not. Everything else you've said has been lies.' Memories of the last time they'd made love, the tender words of Italian he'd whispered to her, slipped into her mind and she realised they too must have been lies.

She turned from him and closed her eyes against the pain. She'd opened her heart to him, given herself and her love, only to find he'd used her as a scapegoat. Behind her, his silence confirmed everything she thought and, despite the pain, she had to hear it all. Maybe then she'd stop loving him.

Purposefully, she returned to the table, pulled out another chair and sat down. She was going to get to the bottom of this if it was the last thing she did. Part of her didn't want to hear it, didn't want to accept that her brother had become embroiled in such a world. But she had to know—everything.

'I saw the report, Sandro.' He didn't say anything but his firm gaze held hers.

'Giovanni told me, or rather confirmed, about the drink…' her breath hitched in her throat and she could hardly form the words as she sat at the table with him '…and drugs. Why didn't you?'

He leant forward in the chair, his elbows resting on his knees and his hands clasped together. His expression was one of concern as he looked up at her and his eyes met hers. 'It was what your father wanted.'

She shook her head. 'Don't use my father. He would never keep such a thing from me.' Even as she said the words she recalled the brief call she'd made to him at the airport. The silence as she'd challenged him. He hadn't admitted anything, but his silence had been deafening.

'Have you spoken to him?'

'At the airport, yes.' She looked into his eyes and the fight began to slip from her, receding like the tide going out. 'I don't understand why he'd do that.'

'He didn't want you to know. He wanted to

keep your memories of Seb untainted.' The gentleness of his voice was almost too much and she shook her head rapidly, wanting to deny everything she was hearing. Her father might have wanted to protect her, but what about Sandro? What were his motives?

'And what about you? Why did you lie to me?' Fierceness exploded from deep within her, a need to shield herself from the fallout of his deceit.

'What do you think would have happened if the press had found out?' His firm question almost knocked the breath from her as she realised the implications of what he said. Shock sank in, washing away the strength she'd just found, and he reached out and took her hand.

Her gaze darted to his tanned hand covering hers, the dusting of dark hair which disappeared under the cuff of his shirt. She could feel the heat from his touch infusing her, awakening all she wished to suppress.

She pulled her hand from under his at the same time as jumping up from her chair, making it scrape noisily on the marble floor. 'What would the press do?' She gulped the words out, hardly daring to form an answer to that question.

'What would they do with a story like that, Charlie?' He sat back in his chair, all cool, calm sophistication, but the glittering hardness of his eyes told her he knew exactly what they would do.

'That's easy,' she retaliated harshly. 'They'd ruin your reputation.'

He stood up, his body full of restraint and composure, but ice had filled his eyes, chilling her to the core. 'Whatever you may think, Charlotte, I have done nothing wrong.'

'You lied—to me and the world.'

'Damn you, don't you see?' He strode towards her, his face full of anger, the angles sharp. 'I wasn't protecting myself. I was protecting Seb—and you.'

In exasperation he flung his hands up and marched towards the gleaming car and, before she could say anything more, he turned to look at her across the room, but it might as well have been across a continent.

The first bubbles of anger rose up like a shaken bottle of champagne and her breathing deepened, but still she couldn't find her voice. How could he stand there and use Seb again, after all that had happened?

Just like she'd seen happen on the podium, the champagne burst out, showering her with fizzy drops of anger. 'How dare you hide behind my brother's reputation after engineering that photo of us kissing? Right here.' She pointed at the car as she crossed the floor to him, her footsteps hard and forceful. 'That photo alone was enough to clear your name. That kiss absolved you of any blame and now it's splurged all over the papers and probably the Internet too.'

He looked taken aback by her outburst but he didn't move. He stood tall and strong as she moved closer and closer, stoking the fiery anger higher and higher.

'I didn't force you to kiss me.' His cool words poured cold water over the flames and for a moment she just looked at him. She couldn't answer that, couldn't offer any defence, because he was right. He hadn't forced her. She had wanted that kiss so badly.

'You manipulated the situation.'

'By "the situation" I assume you mean the heated passion that raged between us from the moment we met?' Suddenly the frozen depths of his eyes heated, so intense they almost scorched her skin.

'That was just a convenient smokescreen.' Despite the bravado, her voice trembled—and she hated herself for it.

She should never have given in to the heady desire that had filled her body and starved her heart. Somewhere deep down she was sure she'd known that, but at the time she'd known she would regret not tasting the desire which had been between them from the beginning. She hadn't wanted to spend the rest of her life wondering *what if?* Now she was going to have to live with the fact that not only had she been used so callously, she'd fallen in love with the man who'd lied and cheated his way into her heart.

Alessandro saw the emotions play out across her face like a movie. Shock, denial, hatred. They were all there. Even passion and longing, but not once did he see anything which resembled what he felt for her.

'So you don't deny it existed.' It was like walking a tightrope. At any moment he could lose his balance and fall. He held his nerve, calling on every bit of control he had. 'You don't deny you wanted me when we kissed right here.'

She looked at him, her eyes saying things he hoped were true but her lips stony silent. He moved forward but she stayed rooted to the spot.

'Don't run from the passion which exists between us, *cara*.'

'I don't need to run from that. I can handle the passion.' Finally words tumbled from her with a force so fierce he drew in a sharp breath. 'But it wasn't passion, Sandro. It was lust.'

He remained still and silent, sensing there was more, but right now she was visibly shaking with emotions so powerful. He watched her beautiful face as she closed her eyes against them, her long lashes spreading across the paleness of her skin. His heart twisted and it was all he could do not to reach for her and hold her against him.

'Lust I can deal with.' She spoke again, her voice firm and resolute. 'What I want to run from is your deceit.'

'My deceit?' He knew what she was referring to and regret piled on top of the guilt because he hadn't had the strength to find a way to tell her everything. This guilt was intensified because he'd pushed aside the promises he'd made to spend the weekend with her, to indulge the lust, as she called it.

'You lied to me, kept the truth from me, then used the spark of lust which was there, even at my cottage, to lure me to the launch night. To this very spot, and engineer the photograph that would prove to the world my family had forgiven you.'

Slowly he shook his head. How was he ever

going to prove he had nothing to do with the photo, that it was just a lucky shot for the photographer? 'I know how it must look,' he began, but she cut his words off.

'What would Seb say if he knew what you have done, how you tricked me so cruelly? What would he say about us?'

A glimmer of hope trickled through him at her mention of 'us' and he gave voice to the conclusion he'd reached just a few hours ago. 'Maybe it was what he wanted all along.'

'How can you know that? Much less say it.' She turned from him and for a moment he thought she was going to walk away. He knew he couldn't go after her again. As she stood, lost in thought, he moved towards her cautiously.

'Seb made me promise to look after you,' he said softly and saw her shoulders rise and fall with each breath she took. 'Not just that night after the accident, but several times before. He played on my loyalty to my sister.'

'That doesn't mean anything.' She turned her head slightly and he saw her profile as she looked distractedly at the floor. Pain and hurt lingered on her face.

Her voice trembled and finally she turned to look at him and, like the moment he'd unveiled the car, he saw her with all her vul-

nerabilities exposed, all her barriers down.
'You should still have told me about the drink
and the drugs. I had a right to know. I don't
care about anything else, not even that stupid photo, but that was the one thing you
shouldn't have kept from me. Not even because of a promise.'

He fought really hard against the urge to
hold her, to soothe all the pain, but right now
he didn't dare. If she ran again it would be for
ever; he knew that much.

'Seb was beside himself, desperate that you
should never know, and I made the promise
to keep him calm. By the time your father
arrived I was firmly fixed into it. I'm sorry,
Charlotte. I had no choice at all.'

As he spoke he thought of why he was here,
what had made him race to the airport in the
first place. All he'd been able to think about
was taking her in his arms and holding her,
comforting her as he had that night in his office. He should have told her the truth then but
she'd been too fragile, so he'd kept the secret.

How did you tell the woman who had just
kissed you with such passion news like that?
Selfishly, he'd kept silent, enjoying the spark
that had been lit between them. Now he knew
that spark wasn't just lust, not for him at least.
It was love.

He loved her. He didn't just desire her—he loved her, so much it hurt.

He needed Charlie, or Charlotte, as he thought of her, when passion blazed in her eyes. She was Charlie behind the wheel of a car and Charlotte in his arms, and he loved her—completely and unconditionally.

Charlie thought of what Alessandro had just said, the situation he'd been forced into. He had kept that promise to Seb. He hadn't been the one who had told her the truth, so did that make the whole situation any more honourable?

She closed her eyes against the pain of finally knowing the truth and the knowledge that it was time to move on, time to leave her garden of sanctuary and live life as Seb would have wanted her to do. As the realisation dawned, Alessandro put his arms around her and pulled her close. This was where she wanted to be, in the arms of the man she loved, but that still didn't mean he loved her. He'd agreed to her terms of 'not for ever' as they'd stood in his apartment on that first night, had even taken her away to his villa to enable him to distance the affair from everything else.

'Why are you here, Sandro?' She looked

up at him, hardly daring to hope. But he *was* here, holding her so tenderly—didn't that mean something?

'I couldn't let you go, not without explaining.' His face was full of concern, but she searched for more, desperate to find even a trace of something else.

'So, *cara*. Why are *you* here?' The term of endearment, said in the most gently seductive tone, gave her just enough hope. 'You know the truth yet you are still in my arms.'

She looked up at him, wondering if he'd see the reason shining from her eyes. He'd been protecting her from the truth all along. She didn't hate him. She loved him. He had honoured Seb's promise at great cost to himself and that just made her love him even more, but could she say those words aloud?

'I couldn't go, not yet.' She lowered her lashes, not wanting to see what was in his eyes, not daring to hope. 'I needed the truth.'

Was it her imagination or had his arms loosened slightly around her? She swallowed hard and took a deep breath.

'And now that you have it?' He let go of her, walked towards the car, pressing his palm against the fiery red paintwork. 'Now that you know the truth, will you return to your life, move on?'

It was as if he was letting her go, allowing her to walk away and find her destiny. Did he not know *he* was her destiny? That if he didn't want her she didn't have a life to return to? She couldn't stop her limbs from trembling and couldn't find the words to tell him what he needed to know.

'Sandro, I...' Her shaky voice deserted her; she began to feel suffocated, as if she couldn't get enough breath into her lungs.

He looked over at her, his brow furrowed into a frown, but it was his eyes that finally showed her what she needed to see. His gaze darted to her as her words died as she saw it. In the dark depths she saw the same hopelessness which filled her heart and she knew she had to say those words. With a jolt she also realised why he wouldn't say them first.

I don't do for ever.

Her words on that first night they'd made love drifted through her mind like a haunting spirit. 'Sandro, I have to say this. I can't go without telling you.'

Slowly she walked towards him, her heart pounding so hard in her chest she almost couldn't think. He looked away from her and jabbed his fingers through his hair, turning his body away, deflecting anything she might try to say. Had she misread the hope in his eyes?

'Just go, Charlotte. If that's what you want to do, there is nothing more to say.' She saw his jaw tense as he gritted his teeth, felt the raw pain and knew she hadn't misread anything.

'I love you, Sandro.' The silence that suddenly shrouded them was so heavy she almost couldn't stand and for a moment he didn't move, frozen in time.

When he did, it was such a small movement, disbelief all over his face as he stepped towards her. In slow motion he reached for her hands, taking them in his and drawing her towards him. She was desperate for him to speak, to say something, but he just looked at her, his hands firmly wrapped around hers.

'Ti amo, ti amo...' His seductive accent caressed each word and his lips, which had moments ago been pressed into a hard line, smiled. Wonder and happiness sparked from his eyes and she fell into his embrace, feeling as if she had come home. She'd found where she needed to be to move on in life.

Right here in the arms of the man she loved.

* * * * *

LARGER-PRINT BOOKS!
GET 2 FREE LARGER-PRINT NOVELS PLUS
2 FREE GIFTS!

⊕ HARLEQUIN®

Romance

From the Heart, For the Heart

YES! Please send me 2 FREE LARGER-PRINT Harlequin® Romance novels and my 2 FREE gifts (gifts are worth about $10). After receiving them, if I don't wish to receive any more books, I can return the shipping statement marked "cancel." If I don't cancel, I will receive 4 brand-new novels every month and be billed just $5.09 per book in the U.S. or $5.49 per book in Canada. That's a savings of at least 15% off the cover price! It's quite a bargain! Shipping and handling is just 50¢ per book in the U.S. and 75¢ per book in Canada.* I understand that accepting the 2 free books and gifts places me under no obligation to buy anything. I can always return a shipment and cancel at any time. Even if I never buy another book, the two free books and gifts are mine to keep forever.

119/319 HDN GHWC

Name _____ (PLEASE PRINT) _____

Address _____ Apt. # _____

City _____ State/Prov. _____ Zip/Postal Code _____

Signature (if under 18, a parent or guardian must sign) _____

Mail to the **Reader Service:**
IN U.S.A.: P.O. Box 1867, Buffalo, NY 14240-1867
IN CANADA: P.O. Box 609, Fort Erie, Ontario L2A 5X3

Want to try two free books from another line?
Call 1-800-873-8635 or visit www.ReaderService.com.

* Terms and prices subject to change without notice. Prices do not include applicable taxes. Sales tax applicable in N.Y. Canadian residents will be charged applicable taxes. Offer not valid in Quebec. This offer is limited to one order per household. Not valid for current subscribers to Harlequin Romance Larger-Print books. All orders subject to credit approval. Credit or debit balances in a customer's account(s) may be offset by any other outstanding balance owed by or to the customer. Please allow 4 to 6 weeks for delivery. Offer available while quantities last.

Your Privacy—The Reader Service is committed to protecting your privacy. Our Privacy Policy is available online at www.ReaderService.com or upon request from the Reader Service.

We make a portion of our mailing list available to reputable third parties that offer products we believe may interest you. If you prefer that we not exchange your name with third parties, or if you wish to clarify or modify your communication preferences, please visit us at www.ReaderService.com/consumerchoice or write to us at Reader Service Preference Service, P.O. Box 9062, Buffalo, NY 14240-9062. Include your complete name and address.

HRLP15